FIGHTING FOR MARI

Redemption Harbor Security Series, #6

Katie Reus

Cover art by Sweet 'N Spicy Designs
Editor: Julia Ganis
Proofreader: Book Nook Nuts
Author website: www.katiereus.com

Dedication

To Allison Lensink, fabulous CFI and friend!

GLOSSARY

ABEAM: An aircraft is "abeam" a fix, point, or object when that fix, point, or object is approximately 90 degrees to the right or left of the aircraft track. Abeam is a general position rather than a precise point.

ADS–B: a performance–based surveillance technology that is more precise than radar and consists of two different services: ADS–B Out and ADS–B In. ADS-B Out works by broadcasting information about an aircraft's GPS location, altitude, ground speed and other data to ground stations and other aircraft, once per second.

AGL: Above Ground Level (as opposed to MSL aka Mean Sea Level).

ALNOT: An 'alert notice' aka a request originated by a Flight Service Station (FSS) or an air route traffic control center (ARTCC) for an extensive communication search for overdue, unreported, or missing aircraft.

ATC: Air Traffic Control

CAPS: In the book I refer to a parachute system while Mari and Colin are in the Cirrus. The official name of that system is The Cirrus Airframe Parachute System (aka CAPS). It is a parachute system that deploys from a Cirrus aircraft in an emergency.

CFI: Certified Flight Instructor

CTAF: Common Traffic Advisory Frequency

FSS: Flight Service Station (Flight Service provides pilots with weather and aeronautical information through pilot briefings, flight planning, inflight advisory services, weather cameras, search and rescue initiation, aircraft emergencies, and Notices to Airmen (NOTAMs).)

IFR: Instrument Flying Rules

NTSB: National Transportation Safety Board. The NTSB is an independent federal agency that investigates civil aviation accidents in the United States as well as significant events among other modes of transportation (trains, etc.)

TAS: Traffic Advisory System. TAS is an advisory-only system that alerts pilots to nearby traffic. (TAS also stands for true airspeed, but that is not how the acronym was used in this book.)

TCAS: A traffic alert and collision avoidance system designed to reduce the incidence of mid-air collisions between aircraft.

VFR: Visual Flying Rules

7500 squawk code: used by pilots to discreetly indicate that their aircraft is experiencing a hijacking or unlawful interference.

7700 squawk code: used by pilots to indicate a general aircraft emergency.

CHAPTER 1

Every takeoff is optional. Every landing is mandatory.

"Hey, how're you feeling?" Mari answered via her car's Bluetooth as she zipped through the monstrosity of New Orleans traffic.

"Good, why?" Magnolia, her best friend since forever asked in clear confusion.

"Uh, because you're pregnant!" Magnolia already had a seventeen-year-old son with her new husband, though he'd been out of their lives for the last eighteen-ish years. All because of someone's lies. But they were back together and now expecting a baby, and Mari was ridiculously happy for her.

"Oh, right." Magnolia snort-laughed. "I forget sometimes. I mean, I don't *actually* forget, but...oh my god, that's not why I'm calling. I heard from a little birdie that you're playing with fire."

"That could mean so many things." Mari laid on her horn when the guy in front of her—clearly on his phone—didn't go when the light turned green.

"Did you swipe one of Colin Lockhart's clients?"

Now Mari snort-laughed. "Not quite, but I did snag some land I know he was looking at." She hadn't even wanted it, but he'd stolen one of her clients, so whatever. Payback, baby. He was going to learn that he didn't always get his way.

"Land for what?"

"Some acreage up in north Louisiana. Got it for a steal too. In the next year or so it'll be another one of my airports." She had a handful in her portfolio. All small airports within seventy miles of major ones. None of them had towers, and they were basically places for people who wanted to fly into certain areas with a bit more privacy than large airports, and even some private ones, afforded. "I won't even have to do much clearing for the runway."

"Hmmm."

"What's that mean?" She laid on the horn again.

"Oh my god, you use your horn more in one day than I do all year."

"I reserve it for assholes on their phone...and I realize that I'm on my phone. But I'm not texting or looking at it. I'm using the hands-free option."

Magnolia sighed. "I'm not having this conversation again with you." But there was laughter in her voice.

"So who's this little birdie you've been talking to?"

"Bear."

"Oh, that's fine then. What did he say?" she asked like they were still in high school instead of women closer to forty than thirty. But Mari wanted to know because she adored Bear. Wasn't his fault that his brother Colin was an assface.

"Not much, just that you and Colin were going at it again."

Okay, there was no *going at it* or *again*. But there was a healthy dose of competition between them that Colin could blame on himself. He never should have stolen that client from her. Because Mari Kim held a grudge.

Something she'd learned at a young age from her halmeoni. You mess with a Kim, expect payback.

"How is Bear? I haven't talked to him since he and Valentine moved into their new home."

"I know you're changing the subject, but fine. He's great, adorable. They're thinking of getting married in the same place Ezra and I did." There was a wistful note to Magnolia's voice.

"I love that." As she headed to the Lakefront Airport, she and Magnolia talked right up until she parked and finally had to go. Friday was one of her busier days and normally she was at the airport at least an hour before she had to take off, but she was cutting it close today. Luckily her client was always running late.

But of course by the time she made it to the hangar, her oldest and favorite client Gary Sewall was talking to another pilot she knew close to the bay door.

She absolutely looooved his plane, but at close to two million dollars new—and about a hundred thousand annual operating costs—it was never happening for her personally. But she got to fly it weekly, which was incredible. The interior felt like a sedan more than anything, with butter-smooth leather seats, illuminated cupholders, subtle accent lights and enough storage for most people. And forget about the cockpit dash, it was a dream to fly.

"Hey, you're late." Gary's tone was light as he strode over the concrete to meet her.

"I'm thirty minutes early."

"Which translates to late for you."

"And you're early, so clearly we've changed places today."

He laughed that booming laugh that had taken her a while to get used to. "Fair enough. So why are you *not* late this morning?"

"Had to sign some paperwork for a small land purchase," she said as she fell in step with him.

His Berluti oxfords made soft clicking sounds as they walked the expanse of the hangar. His plane was at the back because he liked to keep it tucked away from everyone else's. The truth was he could probably just buy his own hangar, but she was pretty sure he liked to show it off. And she couldn't blame him. "Another airport?" he asked.

"Maybe. We'll see." She sometimes talked business with him, but she'd also learned years ago to keep most of her private life to herself. Clear boundaries were just as important in business as they were in her personal life.

"I'll find out. I always do."

She snickered but her laugh faded as she reached the newer Cirrus to find another man waiting nearby, looking impatiently at her.

"If this is an example of your work ethic, then this isn't going to work out," the stranger said.

Blinking, she looked at Gary. "What's happening right now?"

He sighed, his expression tight as he nodded at the man in a suit similar to his own. Custom and expensive. "Mari, this is, Jeremy Ackerman, a business associate of mine. We're headed to the same place today so I figured he could hitch a ride with us."

It was his plane and his dime. "Sure. I just need to do the preflight check—"

"We're already running late, so we can skip all that and just go." The man made as if he was about to get into the plane.

Oh, hell no. "Sir, I will do the preflight check or we're not leaving." It didn't matter how well you knew your plane or how often you flew it. Preflight was one of the most important things a pilot did and had saved countless lives. She didn't cut corners when it came to safety measures, not even for rich, arrogant assholes. Her very first CFI—Certified Flight Instructor—had drilled that into her years ago. Ignoring basic safety was how people died.

To her surprise, the man chuckled and grinned at Gary. "You told me she was no-nonsense."

Gary glanced at her sideways, his expression apologetic.

Oh jeez, this was some weird test? Mari kept her expression neutral as the man held out his hand, but she took it out of politeness, shaking it.

"I was just messing with you. Take your time. Gary knows I'm looking for a new pilot and offered to let me fly with you today."

"Sounds good." She kept her expression in that same neutral she'd mastered over the years—she'd had to with her parents. She loved them, but they were a lot, and her being a private pilot had never been on their life plan for her. According to them, she could have and *should* have been a doctor. Apparently it didn't matter that the sight of needles made her want to puke.

After she finished the preflight without issue and confirmed with ATC, they headed out into clear skies.

Once they were in the air and a few miles out, Gary finally spoke into the headset. "Jeremy really is looking for a new pilot. He flies back and forth up north a lot like me, but on different days—which is why I don't mind sharing your time."

Mari nodded even as she monitored a couple nearby planes on the dash. But they were all well above them at this point. "Sounds good. How're you doing back there, Jeremy?" He was in the back of the Cirrus, which rode like a luxury sedan.

"Great. That was a smooth takeoff."

"Thanks."

"Hopefully the landing is just as smooth."

"Absolutely." She wasn't sure how else to respond to this guy. Normally she had no problem with small talk, but the way he'd "tested" her at the beginning by being a jerk had set the tone and she was still annoyed. Maybe irrationally so, but...she did hold a grudge.

"So how long have you been flying?"

She had a feeling the guy already knew the answer, but went along with it. "Almost twenty years."

"You don't look old enough to have been flying that long."

Yeah, she got that a lot. She was five foot one and still got carded sometimes, which felt over-the-top, but whatever. There were certainly worse things in life. "Yeah, I got lucky with my genes," she said lightly. "So tell me about you, if you don't mind." In her experience, rich guys loved to talk about themselves. "What are you looking for specifically?"

And she'd been right, because that was all it took. He talked for most of the flight about his job as a "curator of interesting things," and his family, including his daughter, and that was his only saving grace in her opinion. Because it was clear he was a good dad, loved his kid and was proud of her.

People had layers, and while this guy had rubbed her the wrong way at first, maybe he wasn't so bad.

"We're staying here this weekend," Gary said when they were about fifteen miles out from the small airport in northern Louisiana that he preferred.

"Fun plans?"

He snorted, but Jeremy answered before Gary could. "What happens on the road stays on the road. Right, Gary?"

She was glad she was facing forward so he couldn't see her expression. Maybe he was a douche after all—first impressions really were spot on more often than not.

"Should I pick you up Monday?" she asked Gary.

"I'll let you know. Might be Tuesday. Just depends." He sounded exhausted by that, which wasn't surprising. He worked as a political consultant and his hours were wild. It seemed like he was always working. Even on the flight here, he'd been on his tablet eighty percent of the time.

"Sounds good. I'm teaching a few classes and doing a couple intro flights at the school, but you know how to reach me." She'd switched from corporate pilot to contract pilot not too long ago so now she made her own hours and chose her own clients. Gary had moved with her when she made the switch, though nothing between them had changed. Now she was able to work at a local flight school more and volunteer with the chapter of an international aviation group to get young girls excited about aviation, something she loved.

After indicating the airport name and the Cirrus's flight call sign, she continued her ATC call, "...ten miles requesting the visual for runway three six, full stop."

As she got into the pattern, then eventually moved into the final approach, she tuned out everything else as years of training kicked in.

"Perfect," Gary said once they were on the taxiway, rolling toward the small airport building. This one wasn't as big as the one in New Orleans, but they had killer kimchi burritos and she was going to grab one while the plane was being fueled up.

"I'll be in touch soon," Ackerman said to her as they reached the small rectangular building. "I'm also talking to Colin Lockhart. His business is newer than yours, but he flew in the military, so." He shrugged and she couldn't read his meaning.

"Okay, sounds good," she said, not wanting to take the bait. But she was every bit as good as Colin, military service or not.

"It's clear that you're a great pilot, but I just want to make sure I find the right fit."

"I don't take on every person who reaches out to me either, so I totally get that." She could decide who she wanted to fly or not.

He nodded, her meaning flying right over his head—pun intended. "Lockhart had some interesting things to say about you."

Interesting? That sounded like code for something asshole-ish and all she could think about were the things Colin had said about her when they were younger. When he hadn't known she could overhear him.

She turned away from Ackerman. "Gary, I hope you have a great weekend. Let me know when you need me. I'll take care of your baby on the way home, but before I leave I'm about to grab a burrito."

"Don't lie, you know you're getting three," he said, already on his tablet again, grinning and shaking his head.

She laughed because he wasn't wrong. She always grabbed a couple to go then ate them throughout the week. Her mom really was right: she had the palate of a twelve-year-old. Though to be fair these flavor bombs had black beans, rice and other veggies packed in, so she was totally getting more good stuff in addition to the kimchi. "Have a good one." She waved at the two of them before heading inside to grab her food—all while trying to shove down her growing annoyance.

Colin had interesting things to say about her, did he?

She took a deep breath and forced herself to relax. There was no sense in getting all riled up, but...he had already swiped one of her clients. Would he really trash-talk her to potential clients just to keep them himself?

The pilot world was small and she already had to fight to be taken seriously because of her gender—women made up only seven percent of pilots in the world. And in the US, she was pretty sure it was only five percent. She'd be damned if she'd let Colin Lockhart tarnish her hard-won reputation.

As she ordered, she debated calling him and asking about what Ackerman had said, but decided she was going to pay him a visit instead. Just as soon as she got back to the city.

Chapter 2

When life gives you crosswinds, apply rudder pressure.

Colin glanced up from his computer as Mari Kim stalked into his office looking as if she was ready to pick a fight. Which was basically her expression all the time around him.

Not around others though. Oh no, she smiled for everyone else, it seemed.

And he was her brother's best friend. Once upon a time they'd been friends too. Or friendly. But then for whatever reason she'd decided she hated him.

And just an hour ago he found out that she'd swiped a land deal out from under him. Which, fine—business was business. But he knew this was personal for her, which made the swipe even more annoying.

"Please, come on in," he said dryly as she marched to the front of his desk and sat down in one of the chairs as if she owned the place.

She crossed her legs, looking way too smug. And he hated how much he liked that expression on her. To be fair, he liked everything about the woman. She was all wild energy and confidence, and it was one of the sexiest things. He'd never met anyone like her. "How's business?"

He narrowed his gaze slightly as he leaned back in his chair. He worked with two other pilots—both former military like him—and they were thankfully not here to see whatever this was because they'd give him shit about it forever. Unlike Mari, who was strictly a contract pilot who took jobs, he'd created a company with contracting and teaching in mind. If he didn't think she'd kick his teeth in, he would offer her a job. Or hell, a partnership. He'd be lucky to get to work with someone of her skills.

But that was very much off the table. "Good. Why are you here?"

"Spoke to Jeremy Ackerman today." There was something in her tone he couldn't quite read.

"Okay. And?"

She narrowed her dark eyes at him and leaned forward slightly. In a simple gray T-shirt, jeans, and blue and yellow sneakers, she looked like she always did. Gorgeous. Her dark hair was pulled up in a short ponytail—she'd recently cut off about eight inches and looked even more stunning.

"He said you had *interesting* things to say about me."

Interesting? "I told him that you have a good reputation, tons of repeat clients, and that when you went fully contract a bunch of your clients followed you."

She snorted, clearly not believing him. Which annoyed the hell out of him.

"You don't believe me?"

"He made it sound like you were saying unflattering things about me."

Yeah, well Jeremy Ackerman had been a jackass and not someone Colin wanted to work with, so he actually believed the guy had insinuated something else. "Well, I didn't. I would never do that. Your reputation speaks for itself anyway." And if Ackerman couldn't see that, that was on him.

She shoved up from the chair, her expression still disbelieving. "Sure." As she stormed out of his office, Oliver, one of his partners, walked in.

His way too good-looking friend of almost twenty years did a sideways glance at Mari as she strode past him. He wanted to tell Ollie to keep his eyes to himself, but then his friend said, "Hey, got a sec?"

Nope. "Hold on. Mari, slow down!" He hurried out into the hangar—his office was at the back of the hangar tucked away out of sight, but for the most part the hangar was always open.

She ignored him, moving fast for someone so short. She'd always been like that, a ball of energy who never quit.

"What the hell is your problem with me?" he demanded as he caught up to her.

"So many things," she growled as they stepped out into the sunshine and she slid her aviators on. She still didn't look at him, simply kept going toward the attached parking lot.

He gritted his teeth. He was sick of her hostility. He'd done nothing to deserve it.

"Hey, Colin!" Gino, one of his other partners, called out as he jogged across the parking lot.

Colin ignored him, following Mari to her Jeep. "Seriously, Mari, can you hold on?"

At her door, she turned to look up at him. Then she jumped up onto the running board so she was taller than him. Because of course she did. "What?"

"What's your problem with me? Why the hell would you think I'd talk trash about you to some stranger? Or to anyone for that matter," he gritted out, even though he was trying to stay calm. It bothered him more than he wanted to admit that she could think that about him. He loved her whole family.

"Well it wouldn't be the first time." She ducked into her Jeep and slammed the door in his face as he stood there blinking at her.

Wait, what? But she was already pulling out of her spot.

And short of jumping onto the back of her vehicle and clinging to the spare tire like a lunatic, this conversation was clearly over.

"Damn, who was that?" Gino jogged up next to him, his gaze following after Mari's Jeep.

"None of your damn business," he growled, stalking back to the hangar.

"Oooh, so was that Evan's sister Mari, then?"

Colin shot him a sharp glance.

"I'm not asking because she's Korean." He held his palms up. "I'm asking because you have that same look... You know what? Never mind, I don't even want to get involved in whatever this is. I'm meeting a potential new student here in half an hour, so I'll be in the hangar if you need me."

Irrationally annoyed—at everything—Colin pulled out his cell and texted Evan, Mari's oldest brother. *You free tonight?*

Yeah. Want to come over for dinner? Carmen's mom is making paella tonight so there'll be plenty.

I'll be there. He didn't even have to think twice. Evan's mother-in-law had recently moved into their guest house and she'd taken to cooking for the family more nights than not. Even if she wasn't cooking, he'd be there. Because he was done with this and wanted answers.

***

Colin cleared his own plate as well as the others as Carmen halfheartedly protested. "You guys invited me over. Sit." He also needed a moment away from Evan and Carmen as they cuddled against each other on the outdoor seating.

He adored the two of them, was happy his best friend had found the woman for him. But every time he saw them together so ridiculously in love, it reminded him that he was alone. Which he'd never cared about until recently.

He'd lived a full life and had no regrets, but now that he was back in New Orleans, near Mari…he couldn't help but think about "what if." So damn many what-ifs where she was concerned. He'd wanted her forever, but she'd made it clear she didn't feel the same.

So he'd had to box up his feelings and pretend they didn't exist. And he'd never said anything to anyone, not even Evan.

But that box he'd closed up tight had popped open and he was having a hard time putting the lid back on. Wasn't even sure he wanted to anymore.

He loaded up the dishwasher and only left the kitchen once Carmen's mom came in and actually shooed him out with a dishrag.

"This is why you're always welcome," Carmen said with a laugh when he came back out with a pitcher of water and topped her off. "And I know you cleaned up the kitchen."

"Until your mom kicked me out."

"I don't know how she has more energy than me."

"Probably because you're growing a human." Evan kissed the side of her head.

She laughed lightly, then stood up, stretched. "I'm going to keep my mom company while you two talk about whatever it is you came by to talk about." She gave Colin a pointed look before heading back inside.

"That woman is psychic." He stretched his legs out in front of him as he looked out at the sparkling pool.

"Probably, but it doesn't take a psychic to know something's up. What's going on? You've been tense all night."

Now Colin was second-guessing himself, but shoved that aside. "Mari stopped by the hangar today and was angry at me." Something he was still annoyed about since he hadn't done anything to deserve her ire.

Evan snorted. "What's new?"

"No, this was different. She thought I was essentially talking shit about her to this potential client. So what's the deal? I've never pushed before, but why does she dislike me so damn much?" Or hate him. But he couldn't make himself say the word. Even if she swore she did for reasons he couldn't fathom.

Evan paused for a moment, glanced out at the glittering pool. Their neighborhood was in the Garden District and was relatively quiet most of the time, tonight no exception. "I don't know," he finally said. "I think it's just you both have strong personalities. That's all."

Colin was pretty sure his friend was holding something back, but wasn't going to push. Normally he would since they were best friends, but Mari was Evan's sister. There was a line he didn't want to cross. He certainly wouldn't want to talk about his brother to anyone so he understood. "Okay."

But Evan continued. "My sister holds a grudge, that's all I'll say. So while it might be a personality thing...she also might be angry about something. She shaved Joseph's eyebrows right before prom because...of something. I don't even remember."

"He dated one of her friends, then broke up with her days before prom to take someone else." Colin liked their younger brother, but figured Joseph had deserved the shaved eyebrows. Probably worse.

"Oh right. Shit, I forgot he did that. Well, at least she never shaved your eyebrows."

Colin laughed lightly, but it was forced. There was no way this was a personality thing. She was angry at him for something specific, had to be. And he was going to figure out what it was and fix their relationship.

CHAPTER 3

If you have a best friend as weird as you, you have everything.

"You have the best job," Mari said to Berlin.

She, Berlin, Camila and Magnolia were all at Magnolia's tonight since Lucas and Ezra were having a Friday night boys' night—aka they were playing basketball at Bradford's with the rest of the Redemption Harbor Security crew and probably gorging themselves on pizza afterward.

"So says the badass pilot." Berlin's eyebrow arched as she picked up her glass of wine.

"Yeah, so says me. I don't get to hack stuff all day."

"Allegedly." Berlin shot Camila a sideways glance.

The detective just grinned. "Yes, *allegedly*. And please don't say anything else about that. I need plausible deniability."

"Especially after your promotion." Magnolia stepped back out onto the patio, a small charcuterie board in hand. They'd already devoured an embarrassing amount of snacks but thankfully her bestie was prepared for them. "And Adalyn is on the way. She said she got caught up with something."

"Let's eat all the cheese balls before she gets here," Berlin said, moving for the tray.

"Hold up, I've got a croquembouche tower of pastries," Magnolia said, laughing. "And another plate of dasik." She looked pointedly at Mari because they were her favorite.

"Forget cheese, I'm going to devour the dasik plate and the entire croquembouche tower." Magnolia had gotten the dasik recipe from Mari's mom and she would be forever grateful because her bestie made the sesame tea cookies all the time for her. And Mari wasn't sure how her best friend made the croquembouche, but she always ate way too much of them. Then wanted more.

"I'll pay you a thousand dollars if you eat that whole tower," Berlin said.

"You're going to be out money." Magnolia's tone was dry as she disappeared back into her house. First she brought out the small tray of dasik, then came out with the croquembouche.

Mari jumped up to follow her and hold open the door as she came back out. "You shouldn't be carrying all this stuff," she said, taking the tray from her—and resisting the urge to shove her face into it. "I'm sorry, I should have offered to get all this." She inwardly chastised herself. Normally Magnolia took over and liked being the hostess, but Mari should have been helping more.

"Yeah, sorry," Camila added, Berlin nodding along. "We're shit friends."

"Oh no, I'm already getting the overprotectiveness from Ezra, you guys can't start too. You've all got to be on my side."

"Too late. I've loved you longer than he has, so I can be overprotective too." They'd become friends in kindergarten over their love of Pokémon trading cards and been through all of the ups and downs of life. Magnolia was the one person she'd always been able to count on to never judge her, to just be there. So sure, she was going to be a little over the top now that her bestie was pregnant for the second time. She'd been there for the first time too and adored her nephew.

"How do I argue with that?"

"You don't." She plucked one of the delicate custard-filled cream puffs from the tower.

"When are we going to start talking baby showers?" Berlin asked as Mari swatted her hand away. "Oh my god, you're an animal." She grabbed one of the pastries with her other hand and shoved it in her mouth. Then she grabbed three of the delicate tea cookies.

"It's too soon for baby showers," Magnolia said, shaking her head.

"Yeah, okay, but we're going to go back to it. Also, I want to hear about Mari's work. Did you land that new client?" Berlin turned to her now.

"Yeah, what happened with that?" Camila held out her fork as a weapon to protect herself as she took one of the pastries.

"Oh, I lost that client. But I did manage to make the best of it."

"Why do you look like you murdered someone?" Berlin asked.

Camila held up a hand. "Don't answer that if you did."

"Oh my god, I didn't commit any crimes. I lost the client I'd told y'all about on our text thread, but I did swipe a land deal from the assface who stole my potential client." She glanced at Magnolia who already knew.

Her friend shook her head.

"What? He deserved it." And Mari didn't feel guilty.

"I still don't know why he makes you so mad. Don't get me wrong, I'll hate him until the day I die for you, but...he doesn't seem awful. And he's Bear's brother. I just can't help but wonder what the deal is between you two." She said the last part in a sort of sing-song, all-knowing voice.

"It's not because of sexual tension or whatever you seem to think it is."

Magnolia made a hmmming sound that annoyed the hell out of her.

"So what's the deal between you and assface, aka Colin Lockhart?" Berlin asked as she and Camila listened raptly.

Mari ignored them, still focused on correcting Magnolia's error in judgment. "It's because he told Grayson Sutton I had an STI when I was seventeen!" she blurted. She'd never told Magnolia about it because her friend had been dealing with way too much back then in the form of an unexpected pregnancy.

"Wait, *what*?" Magnolia sat up in her seat. "You're sure?"

"Oh, I'm sure. I heard him say the words."

"When? Where? Details!"

"And where does he live?" Berlin asked. "Because I'll burn him to the ground. Metaphorically," she added, grinning at Camila.

"Like I said, I was seventeen." And she'd had a monster crush on him at the time, so his words had hurt even more. "He was home on leave visiting with Evan. Some of their other friends were home from college that summer. You remember Grayson?"

"Ah...oh yeah. Tall, blond, played lacrosse? A little younger than them? He was in freshman year of college I think?"

"Yep. He was asking about me, wanting to know if I was single, and Colin told him I had an STI and to stay away from me if he valued his junk. He didn't actually use that word, but whatever." Anytime Mari thought about overhearing that conversation she got angry and hurt all over again. Didn't matter that it had been years ago. What kind of a person made up such vicious lies about someone? It could have destroyed her reputation in high school.

"Oh wow, why didn't you ever say anything?" Magnolia asked.

"Because you were pregnant with Lucas and already dealing with so much. At the time it just hurt too much to talk about anyway. I almost told you a couple years later, but by then I was figuring out my life and had dropped out of college." She'd dropped out to go into flight school and life had taken over. "Then it just didn't matter."

"It seems like it kinda does still matter." Berlin swiped another pastry.

Mari sat back in her seat and nodded. "Yeah, I have a problem with grudges. I know I really should let it go." It was hard to though. His opinion of her had meant a lot back then.

"I don't know, I'd probably hold a grudge too," Camila said. "I'm still pissed at my cousin for stealing my boyfriend in fifth grade."

"This is why I love you guys."

Adalyn walked out the back door onto the patio, her sister Fleur behind her, and the conversation shifted, much to Mari's relief.

She didn't want to talk about Colin, she just wanted to enjoy the evening with her friends—and hopefully convince Magnolia that it was definitely time to start planning her baby shower. The first time around they'd been so young and Magnolia hadn't gotten to do a lot of fun baby-related things.

Mari wanted to make sure that this time Magnolia got the full experience of friends and family celebrating her and her little one.

CHAPTER 4

I hate when people can't let go of the past—debt collectors are the worst.

"You want to tell me what's in that case?" Mari glanced at Bradford as they talked over their headsets. He'd hired her last-minute to fly him to pick up something at a tiny airport in the middle of nowhere. She didn't have any other contract jobs today, though the truth was she'd have made time in her schedule for him or any of the employees of Redemption Harbor Security.

They worked in gray areas helping people who needed it and couldn't always turn to law enforcement. They made their own rules and that was something she respected.

"I mean I could, but this way you have plausible deniability if you're ever questioned about it."

She was pretty sure he wasn't kidding. "Fair enough. So...have you been fitted for your suit yet?'

"For what?"

She glanced at him to see if he was messing with her, but he looked blank.

Frowning, she concentrated on flying her little plane. They were about thirty minutes from New Orleans and the air traffic was going to get heavier soon. "Seriously? For Chance and Berlin's wedding."

"Oh. Right. No, the fitting isn't for a couple more weeks. What about you?"

"Berlin said we can basically wear whatever we want. But Violet suggested that we stick to a color scheme." Berlin had also let Mari know she'd love it if Mari wore her hanbok if she wanted, but she was worried it might be too formal for their wedding. She'd decide later.

"Suggested?" Bradford's tone was dry.

Violet had been the wedding planner for Magnolia's wedding and was intense. Mari and the others had only known her for a few months, but they really liked her. Violet was good at her job and took it seriously. "She very politely *ordered* us."

Bradford snickered and glanced out the window of her 1973 Piper Arrow. Her first plane was pretty much her first love if she was being honest with herself. Which was pretty sad, so she ignored the thought. "Sounds about right."

"So are you and Violet in touch outside of wedding stuff?"

"Since when are you so nosy?" His jaw went a little tight, only making him even more handsome.

He was rough around the edges, with tattooed sleeves, dark hair, perpetual scruff on his face and a very "bad boy" vibe. She could totally see him and the prim and proper Violet together.

"Just making conversation with my friend, that's all."

He snorted. "You're such a liar. Did Berlin put you up to asking? Because she has it in her head that Violet and I are 'perfect for each other.'" His expression said he thought otherwise, and she'd gotten to know him well enough to realize that if he was interested in someone, he'd go for it. So it was a no go on Violet.

But fine, she had told Berlin she'd be sneaky and ask. So much for being sneaky though. "What? You're ridiculous. So, for real, what's in the case?

Is it like, a human head?"

He sort of sputtered. "Seriously? First of all, a human head wouldn't fit in a briefcase that size."

"It would if it was liquified. Or if it'd been cremated."

He gave her a look she could only describe as horrified. Then he opened his mouth, shut it, then looked out the dash window.

She grinned to herself. Then she pressed the radio button and made the call to ATC.

It was Wednesday—a whole five days since she'd seen Colin. Not that she was counting. Though her sister-in-law Carmen had mentioned that he'd been over for dinner at their place. Which wasn't really news, considering Colin and Evan were best friends. She swore she'd never be rid of the man.

Thankfully there weren't many planes on the taxiway and she steered them into the hangar with ease. Once they were inside, they both got out and rolled her plane to its spot, then reversed it in neatly.

By the time she'd finished her post-flight check, he seemed to be over her liquified head talk. "Will I see you this weekend?" he asked after she'd finished.

"Hopefully. I told Berlin I'd try to make it to their barbeque. But I've got flights on Thursday and Friday. My Friday one is pretty standard but sometimes my client needs me to come back Saturday to pick him up early so..." She shrugged. As a contract worker she was flexible with her job. Hell, she was pretty sure it was a prerequisite for pilots to be flexible. And she was paid for her on-call time so it was a win-win for her.

"All right, well I'll be there." He looked as if he wanted to say more, but they both turned at the sound of someone approaching.

She resisted the groan that wanted to escape. Colin was headed their way, his stride determined. And why was everything about him all tall, sexy and capable? He was just wearing jeans and a T-shirt, for the love of pizza. But he wore them really, really well, his T-shirt stretching across his muscular chest and thick biceps. *Ugh.*

"Come on, universe," she muttered to herself.

"What?"

"Nothing. Just...don't look or anything but this guy I know... Never mind." Because she couldn't explain their complicated history in less than twenty seconds and Colin was going to be by her plane soon.

Bradford kept his gaze on her and nodded understandingly. "An ex, huh? Should I fake-kiss you or something? Make him jealous that you're with all this?" He motioned down the length of his body, his expression just a little smug.

"Eww."

His eyebrows kicked up. "Wow. Okay, *hurtful*."

"I just meant a hug is good. And he's not an ex—"

She found her face squished up against his hard chest as Bradford pulled her into a big hug. And fine, she didn't hate that Bradford was objectively good-looking.

But Colin was, ugh, so annoyingly handsome that it didn't even matter. No one held a candle to him. Never had. Over the years she would almost convince herself that she'd built up his looks in her mind, but then she'd run into him at her brother's house and had to face reality.

Bradford stepped back and grinned down at her. "I'll see you this weekend," he said right as Colin stepped up to them. He looked at Colin once and nodded politely before stalking off toward the hangar's bay door, his briefcase in hand.

And apparently she was never going to find out if there was indeed a cremated head inside.

Colin watched Bradford stride away for a couple seconds before he looked back at her. And frowned. Even his frown was sexy, that full mouth making her wonder what he would taste like if they ever kissed. Among other things. And that just annoyed her to no end.

"Who was that?"

"Uh... Why are you here?"

For a moment she thought he would push her on who Bradford was, but he let it go. "I hear you'll be flying Jeremy Ackerman?"

Oh, *that* was what this was about? "Yeah, on a temporary basis anyway." He'd reached out and asked about hiring her.

Since he'd annoyed her so much she'd added what she considered a "jerk tax" to her price, almost doubling her normal rate. And he hadn't balked, which made her think she should have raised it even higher. But she'd also made it clear that they were on a trial period. If she was going to be flying him back and forth to North Louisiana a couple times a week they'd be spending a lot of hours together. It should be pleasant for both of them. If it wasn't, he could find another pilot.

Thankfully he'd been chill about the trial period. So she was chalking up that first day she'd flown him to weirdness. Sure she could hold a grudge but she was able to put things aside for solid jobs.

Colin shoved his hands in his pockets, the little frown pulling at his mouth drawing all her attention to said mouth. Why did his lips have to be all pillowy (was that a thing?) and inviting?

Oh wait, he was talking. "I've heard some less than positive things about the guy."

"Less than positive?"

"That he might be into some shady shit," Colin said bluntly.

She stared up at him, waiting for more. "That's it?"

"I mean, there's more, but yeah, essentially. I looked into him when I thought he might end up being a client and he's been investigated by the Feds."

"I know."

He blinked in surprise.

"I looked into him too. But the investigation was dropped and I won't be helping him transport anything. I'm simply flying him to meetings." She also knew that Ackerman worked with a well-respected aviation company out of Colorado that did most of his domestic flights. "I have a very limited working relationship with him. But thank you for your concern," she added because she wasn't sure if this was a good faith type of warning or something else.

Hoisting her small backpack up, she took a step in the opposite direction and Colin fell in next to her.

"Did you really come all the way down here to warn me about him?"

"I was grabbing lunch at the airport and saw you land."

Oh. She wasn't sure if that made it better or worse.

"But I'd planned to reach out to you anyway."

"Well I'm a big girl and can handle myself."

He let out an exasperated sound as they stepped out into the bright sun. "I know that, but you're still Evan's sister—"

So *that* was what this was about. "Look, I don't need another brother trying to look out for me, especially you," she added, then felt a little mean. "It's hard enough being taken seriously in this field."

He stared down at her in confusion as they walked toward the parking lot.

"How is this a surprise to you? I'm a woman in a wildly male-dominated field... Never mind, Colin." She wasn't going to explain something so basic to him.

"I wasn't thinking about it like that. But yes, I know how hard it is for you—or I can see how hard it is for women in general. It's bullshit what you have to put up with. But that's not why I'm down here talking to you.

I just wanted to give you a heads-up that he might be shady. That's it. And I would warn any of my pilot friends about things that could affect their career or person, so this isn't a gender thing."

"We're not friends." She kept her tone neutral as they reached her Jeep. She didn't want him to think he had any power over her whatsoever, or that she cared one way or another what he thought of her. He'd made his opinion of her known years ago.

"We were at one time."

He was a few years older than her, but yeah, he wasn't wrong. They'd been friendly at least.

She sighed, not wanting to get into it. She had a lot of stuff to do today and an early flight in the morning. "Thank you for the heads-up about Ackerman." She cleared her throat, deciding to smooth things out between them because the aviation world was small. "And I'm hearing good things about your company. If I hear of any potential clients that might be a good fit, I'll send them your way."

He scrubbed a hand over his dark hair, his forearm and biceps flexing with the movement. "Thank you and I'll do the same. But that doesn't answer my question."

"Technically you didn't ask a question." She opened her Jeep's door. "And I really have to go. I'll see you around."

Unlike last week when she'd slammed the door on him, today she shut it normally and tried to tune out his presence—which was basically impossible.

But she didn't look in her rearview as she left, refusing to give in to the annoying impulse. Especially since he'd shown up to warn her about a potential bad actor.

It was hard to get annoyed about that.

Even if she wanted to go on holding her grudge, she knew it wasn't healthy. She was never going to trust Colin, but she could let her own baggage go. For *herself.* There was no point in holding on to it anymore.

And it wouldn't hurt to have a professional relationship with the man. From everything she'd heard, his new company was doing well and clients liked him. Having more relationships in the aviation community was never a bad thing.

"I'm letting this go," she said into the quiet of her Jeep. For her own sanity.

Sighing, she steered onto the highway and headed home. She had stuff to do including visiting her old high school to talk to some of the juniors and seniors about the possibility of aviation as a career. Hopefully she would inspire a few young women to follow her lead.

She needed to be focused on that and not obsessing over the very sexy and capable Colin Lockhart.

Chapter 5

One week later

Mari stepped out of Jeremy Ackerman's plane and breathed in the warm afternoon air. She'd dropped him off yesterday morning and he'd needed to stay longer than originally planned. Since Gary, her normal Friday client, had his own change of plans for their normal Friday drop-off and pickup, it had worked out well.

This "airport" was basically a strip of asphalt next to a couple cornfields along with a couple of hangars and a taxiway area, and was one of the smallest she'd been to. Though she owned one smaller than this where a certain branch of the military practiced their short field takeoffs and landings.

She loved that she got to quietly contribute in a small way to the men and women who served their country. Hell, she loved everything about flying and aviation. Because without this job she would have never known about this tiny place surrounded by acres and acres of green grass and crops. There were so many random areas in the country that were absolutely beautiful and that flying had given her a small peek into.

Leaning against the plane, she checked the multitude of weather apps saved on her phone, frowned at a front that looked as if it was moving in faster than predicted. For the most part she flew IFR—Instrument Flight Rules—but that didn't mean she could fly into a thunderstorm. And that was exactly what they could be facing if they didn't leave soon.

Tucking her phone away, she made her way to a small building she'd discovered was basically a little rectangle with a bathroom and a couple couches that faced a television on the screen. It was a place for people traveling to take a break, do their business, then leave after refueling. Nothing fancy, but it served a purpose.

Ackerman wasn't inside, so she texted him again. Someone always dropped him off and picked him up in a hired car, and he'd told her he was here but...she didn't see him.

She checked the closest hangar and found it mostly empty, save for two old Mooneys that looked circa fifties, which she wanted to check out when she had time.

She texted Ackerman yet again, letting him know about the impending storm on the Gulf Coast and headed to the next hangar. This one had the rolling door closed, but as she got closer, she could hear voices inside.

Shouting.

Frowning, she walked up to the half-open side door and paused.

"If you have a problem with what I'm doing, then maybe we don't need you anymore." The voice was male, but she didn't recognize it.

"I didn't say I have a problem. I just don't like this new direction." That was definitely Ackerman.

"Please remind me when I asked for your opinion. You acquire what I ask for, or you're no longer useful."

There was a long pause, then the clearing of a throat. "I guess I just don't understand—"

"I don't give a shit what you think. You're a tool, so remember that," the other man snapped.

A chill snaked down Mari's spine at the guy's aggressive tone. She backed away from the open door and as she did saw a small camera tucked away in the corner of the awning overhang. Instead of waiting to hear any more, she hurried back to the plane waiting on the taxiway. As she reached it, Ackerman stepped out of the hangar.

She pretended not to see him, instead looking down at her phone. Only when he was hurrying across the asphalt to her a few moments later did she look up. "You ready?" Whatever they had been arguing about, it wasn't her business.

He eyed her almost cautiously. "Are we refueled?"

"Yep."

He gave a tight nod. "In the future, after refueling, please wait in the plane. You don't need to be walking around this property. Understood?" Ice dripped from his voice. And maybe a hard warning.

And yep, she understood perfectly. He was up to shit, and didn't want her finding out. Damn, maybe Colin had been right about him. "Of course." She nodded and slid into her seat as he did the same.

Even though she was rattled, she called on years of training as she prepped for takeoff. There was no actual tower, but she made the call into the ether announcing her takeoff for anyone potentially in the air about to land or just flying nearby.

Once they were airborne, she spoke over the headset. "I'm keeping an eye on the storm over the Gulf. We might have to divert if it moves in too fast."

"That's fine." His words were clipped, the tension in him palpable.

For the rest of the flight he didn't say a single word, which was more unnerving than anything. Instead he worked on his tablet, rustled around in his backpack for a while, then when he put it and the tablet away he simply sat like a statue next to her.

Thankfully, after landing he left almost as soon as the plane came to a stop. He didn't even wait for her to park the plane, simply grabbed his bag and was gone once she got to the taxiway.

While she was grateful he'd taken his sour attitude with him, she couldn't shake the chill that invaded her bones. Whoever she'd overheard him arguing with had sounded angry and even violent.

She hadn't wanted Colin to be right about Ackerman, but he might have been. *Dammit.*

This morning she'd been sure this temporary arrangement was going to work out fine, even with Ackerman being prickly, but today had changed things.

And now she wasn't sure she'd take his next flight request. She didn't need his business and her instinct was telling her that she was better off without a client like him.

CHAPTER 6

"I've got to grab this," Colin murmured to his two partners and their potential new client across from him in the quiet conference room. Normally he would never take a phone call during a meeting like this, but when he saw Mari's name on his screen, his heart kicked up.

She *never* called. He only had her phone number because of Evan—and now he was wondering if this was an emergency about her family. It was the only reason he could think for her to call him.

"Is everything okay?" he asked by way of greeting as he stepped out into the hallway.

"I don't know." There was a tremble in her voice that instantly had him on high alert.

"What's going on?"

"I...honestly don't know." She let out a sigh. "Probably nothing. I just...could you meet up with me? I know it's Saturday and you're likely working, so just later, whenever you can."

"I can meet you now." His partners and client might be annoyed, but he could hear worry, if not fear, in her voice.

"Thank you." Yep, that was definite relief, and it surprised him even more. "I'm at the Crawfish Station."

He knew it. A tiny restaurant in the Quarter that was ridiculously loud. "I'll be there in half an hour."

"I'm in the rear, in one of the booths."

Instead of ducking back into the conference room, he shot off a text to Gino and Ollie telling them a family emergency had come up. Which was close enough to the truth.

With traffic and parking it took way too long for him to make it to the restaurant, but almost forty minutes later he found Mari where she said, sitting in a back booth.

A half-eaten basket of long, soggy french fries sat in the middle of the table and her glass of water was still full.

And she looked actually relieved to see him, a definite first. Now he was really worried.

"Thank you for coming. I'm really sorry to bother you on a Saturday."

He understood her apology because it was one of his busy days. Was likely one of her busy days too. People tended to book intro flights on Saturday to see if they wanted to take lessons or hire his company on a contract basis. Had to be the same for her. "It's no problem. What's going on?"

A server appeared out of nowhere, a pad in hand. "Would you like to order a drink?" The college-aged guy eyed her water and mostly uneaten fries disapprovingly. Probably because she was taking up a table during the busy lunch hour.

"Whatever your specialty beer is," Colin said, pulling out the menu from the holding rack. "And I'll take a BBQ shrimp po'boy, a bowl of gumbo and fries. Can I get it to go though?" Mari was clearly stressed and he wanted to continue this somewhere quieter.

"Of course. Be right back with your drink."

"I feel like a jerk for taking up this table," she said above the noise from the speaker blasting nearby. "I'll leave him a nice tip."

Colin waved it away. "I've got this. Now what's going on?" He couldn't stop his overprotectiveness of her even if he wanted to. She might not like him, but the feeling had never been mutual.

"I flew Ackerman yesterday, my third flight with him since our trial contract."

"Did he do something?" Colin knew that asshole was no good.

She shook her head. "Not exactly. I overheard him talking to someone at this hangar. Nothing really terrible but the guy he was talking to sounded terrifying. Then Ackerman was really weird on the return flight. Didn't talk the entire way back. He made it clear that I shouldn't be walking around that airport at all, which is just weird. Since you said you'd looked into him, I thought you'd have more insight than me."

"Is that the only thing that happened?"

She hesitated, then shook her head. "Okay, this is going to sound paranoid, but this morning when I headed out to work I felt like I was being followed. I had an early intro flight, but not much else on the books since a couple people canceled. When I headed home I felt like I was being followed again. Then at home it kind of looked like some of my stuff had been moved. Nothing overt but I'm particular about my things."

"And put it all together and it definitely feels like something is off."

She shoved out a breath, nodded. "Yeah, it's why I picked this place to meet," she said as the server dropped the beer off, then left. "I asked for this table because of the speaker. I feel like I'm being really paranoid but I also don't want to ignore my gut instinct. So...what did you find out about him? Because my guy made it sound like he was nothing to worry about."

Colin wondered what she meant by "my guy" but ignored that for now. "That he was smuggling drugs to smaller airports, in addition to his legit business."

She blinked once, twice, then groaned. "That's not what I was told. I thought he was investigated for not filling out the right transport forms for antiquities. Really low-level nonsense. Sounded like a competitor trying to jam up his business."

"That's true too. So your guy...?"

"Ah, someone I use to do background checks on potential clients. The ones I fly for contract work. Apparently he didn't dig deep enough."

"To be fair, I used someone who has government contacts."

She cursed under her breath. "The conversation I overheard could definitely have been about drugs. At least we're still on a trial basis. I'll just end things, tell him it doesn't work for my schedule."

Good. "Sometimes guys involved in drugs, even peripherally, can be violent."

She sat back in her seat as the server dropped off his to-go bag and the check. She went to reach for it, but he snagged it and handed it back to the guy along with his card.

"I asked you here," Mari said.

He shrugged. "Now I have dinner for later."

"At least let me pay for my—"

"Just stop. You don't care whether I pay."

"No, I don't." She rubbed her hands over her face. "God, I feel so stupid. And angry! I've been so careful over the last few years not to work with people like this. I should've..."

"What?"

"I have a friend who's essentially in private investigation. She's offered so many times to be my point of contact for potential new clients. But I guess I just got comfortable using the same person and I didn't want to mix friendship and business and... Gah, I've made a mess of things."

"You haven't made a mess of anything. Chances are this won't amount to anything. But I don't like that you think you were followed, or that it felt like someone was in your home. I'm going to follow you back to your place and we'll do a precautionary check, see if we find any listening devices."

Her eyes widened. "You really think that's a possibility?"

"With drug runners? Yeah."

She was silent for a long moment, then was quiet as the server came back with their bill and left again. "Okay, let's check out my place I guess for...whatever might be there."

"We should probably check your car too."

She blinked again and god, he really wanted to kiss her. The thought wasn't exactly out of the blue—he'd had the impulse too many times to count over the years—but it sure as hell wasn't the time.

"Okay. Thank you," she murmured so low he almost didn't hear her over the music.

Once they were outside on the street, he slung an arm around her shoulders.

She jerked slightly, looking up at him warily. "What are you doing?"

"You said it felt like someone followed you home and to work. So if someone did follow you, I want this to look like we're dating."

"Oh. Okay." She was stiff as they walked down the street.

Despite the situation he laughed slightly. "Might work better if you wrap your arm around me too."

"Fine." She might as well be chewing glass as she gritted out the word, but she leaned into him and slid her arm around his waist.

And he liked the feel of her up against him way too much. Didn't matter that the timing sucked.

"I'm at the parking lot off Dauphine."

"I'm not too far from that one. I'll walk you to yours first." He kept an eye out for anyone who looked off, though in New Orleans that could be anyone.

It was a Saturday afternoon so there were more people than normal out and a whole lot of tourists on the streets. Especially since they were in the Quarter. Big band music blasted from a nearby bar and restaurant. A woman at the next shop selling T-shirts, shot glasses and any number of souvenir items was passing out flyers.

Colin kept Mari tucked up against him, glad when people seemed to be giving them a wide berth. Likely because of his *screw with me and find out* expression.

"Did you see anyone who looked strange?" she murmured as they reached her Jeep.

"Define strange." His tone was dry.

She looked up at him in surprise and laughed, and god, he loved the sound. "Like that guy with the creepy harlequin mask?" She mock shuddered. "That's the kind of stuff that needs to be outlawed, not nudity."

He grinned. "You don't have to convince me. I say we need more naked people walking down the streets."

She snickered, her shoulders relaxing with her laughter. It had been a long time since she'd been so relaxed around him and he liked it. But they still had to deal with her current situation. "Drop your keys," he said.

"Uh, what?"

"So I can check the undercarriage."

"Oh... Jeez. Okay." She pulled her keys from her small bag and dropped them.

He ducked down, did a quick visual sweep, then another with his phone video.

"You seem really prepared for this kind of thing," she said as he stood.

"Military stuff." He held out his phone so they could both watch the short video. "No devices that I can see." He was talking about explosive ones, though he decided to not say that out loud. If there was an AirTag or something equivalent, he might not have caught it. "We can check more once we get back to your place."

"Okay, and thank you again."

"You don't have to thank me."

"Pretty sure I do."

She could thank him by telling him why the hell she had such a personal grudge against him, but he wouldn't pressure her for an answer when she needed his help. He just hoped that after this she'd finally realize he wasn't the enemy and open up to him.

But more than that, he wanted to make sure that she wasn't in any real danger.

***

At her place an hour later, Colin motioned for Mari to step out on her front porch with him. They'd checked her home, looking for any potential listening devices or small cameras. She needed a security system, not just a sign outside that said she had one. Something he would push for later.

"I didn't see anything." He stood in front of her on the small walkway that led from the sidewalk to her front porch and patio.

She lived in a quiet neighborhood with limited off-street parking, as was normal in a lot of areas around the city.

"But I don't think it would hurt to have someone come through and check more thoroughly," he added.

Sighing, she shoved her hands in her pockets. "I'm starting to feel really foolish. What if I'm just overreacting to a weird incident?"

He lifted a shoulder. "So what if it's an overreaction? Better that than just ignoring something that could be serious."

"Thank you," she muttered.

"For what?"

"For not making me feel crazy."

He frowned at that. "It's smart that you're trusting your instincts..." He trailed off as she frowned at something behind him. Turning, he saw a dark SUV with tinted windows slowly cruising down her street. "You know them?"

"No, but there's a house for sale at the end of the—"

"Weapon!" He moved into action, scooping her up and running just as the muzzle of a rifle slid out the cracked window.

He sprinted around the side of the house as gunfire splintered the quiet afternoon air, diving behind the air-conditioning unit with her curled up against him. Not much cover but it was all they had as the rapid fire continued.

When there was a pause, he didn't waste time. "Come on." He peered around the edge of the unit, didn't see the SUV anymore so he grabbed her hand. "We've got to get out of here."

Dark eyes wide, she took his hand. They raced through her gated backyard toward the back fence just as another round of gunfire erupted.

CHAPTER 7

Mari couldn't get rid of the chill that had settled in her bones, even sitting in the quiet office of Detective Camila Flores—one of her longtime friends.

Instead of calling 911, she'd called Camila directly. Her friend had shown up at the same time the officers she'd dispatched had. Thankfully she'd taken over while they'd secured the scene.

"Hey, they had mostly junk," Colin said as he stepped into the room. He was holding what looked like coffee and a small bag of something hopefully full of carb goodness.

"Junk sounds good."

He snorted softly. "You're still eating like a twelve-year-old?"

She shrugged but peered into the bag curiously. Two candy bars, four types of chips and Funyuns. She opened them first. Who knew that getting shot at would give her the munchies? She needed comfort in a big way, and since she couldn't have her comfort burrito, this would do for now.

Colin stood at attention between her and the door. "I got the coffee from a cart out front so it's not disgusting. Drink it, it'll warm you up."

"Thanks. I feel so cold and it's driving me crazy."

"You just had a shock."

He seemed perfectly normal, like getting shot at with a semiautomatic weapon wasn't a big deal. "You handled things well." And for that she was grateful. He'd jumped into action so insanely fast while she'd still been processing the word *weapon*. Without him, she'd probably be dead. "Thank you for saving my life."

He sort of grunted, but didn't otherwise respond.

"Want a candy bar?"

He glanced at her, breaking his staring contest with the door. If anyone who wasn't Camila or a good guy opened that door, clearly he was going to take them out. "I'm okay, thanks."

"Your loss." She shrugged. "Did you call my family?"

"No. I figured you'd want to do that."

Mari breathed out a relieved sigh. "I'm not planning on telling them anything yet, so let's just keep this between us." They would lose their shit and she couldn't handle any more stress right now. Her family loved her and she knew she was lucky in that. Her mom might be overbearing, but it came from a loving place and a lived experience that Mari could only try to understand.

"I did text Magnolia."

Mari froze. "What?"

Colin looked completely unapologetic as he finally sat, taking the seat across from her. God, when would Camila come back? She was ready to get out of here and get a little distance from Colin. He smelled amazing and was being so incredibly wonderful. Even the whole "saving her life thing" aside, he was being human and normal, and it was messing with her head. She'd put him in a box where he was this giant asshole for so long and now she was having to reconcile that with who he was right now. When she'd needed him, he'd come. Simple as that.

"Nothing to say?" she continued.

"Like what? I'm not going to apologize. She's your best friend and I figured you would want some support. And let's be real, your detective friend likely called her anyway."

She snickered and dug back into her Funyuns. "I hate the thought of her worrying right now, but you're probably not wrong about that. Thank you."

"Stop thanking me," he growled, and oh god, why did she like that rumbly sound so much?

No. Noooo. A sort of realization hit her square in the chest. One she immediately discarded. She could not deal with any sort of warm, fuzzy feeling when it came to Colin. "Why?"

"Because I don't like it."

"That's not really an answer."

"Well it's all you're getting." Now he was back on his feet and facing the door—away from her.

With him turned away, she got to drink in the lines of his broad shoulders and—noooo. *Stop it*, she ordered herself. She was not attracted to Colin Lockhart. Not even after he had saved her, literally protecting her with his body.

Okay, that was a lie, but she refused to acknowledge it.

Today had just been terrifying, that was all.

"We need to think about where you're going to go after this."

Yeah, she'd thought about that. "I'm going to talk to some of my friends. I think I have a solution." She wasn't going to tell him that her friends with Redemption Harbor Security had safe houses tucked away around the city in quiet little neighborhoods.

"What kind of solution?"

Before she could answer, the door opened and Bradford stepped in, all tall and handsome and very worried. "Hey, short stuff."

"Don't call me that," she grumbled. "Or I'll wipe my Funyun-covered fingers all over your shirt."

He ignored her and pulled her into a tight hug. "Magnolia is worried about you."

"Just Magnolia?" She hugged him back, grateful for the human touch. Though if she was being honest with herself (and no thanks, not right now, reality was overrated), she wanted to be hugging Colin instead. But that wasn't on the menu.

"Hell no. We're all worried." He turned to Colin, who was sort of staring him down, and held out a hand. "And thank you for saving our girl. Camila told me what happened. That was a quick reaction time." Bradford sounded as impressed as she felt.

Colin seemed taken off-guard, but shook Bradford's hand. "I'd do anything for Mari."

His words caught her by surprise, sending a weird spiral of heat through her. She stared at him for a long moment, unsure how to take him. Was there more meaning behind what he'd said? He turned to look at her and she felt her world tilt on its axis, knew that it was never going to be properly aligned again.

So she picked up the coffee he'd bought and took a big swig—and promptly burned her mouth. Yep, that did it. She gasped and set the cup down, glad to have broken whatever weird spell she was clearly under.

"Have you talked to Camila?" she asked Bradford, needing to keep her focus on him and not stare at Colin like a hungry hyena.

"Yeah, I ran into her. She's on her way up."

Colin glanced down at his phone, frowned. "I'll be just outside," he said to Mari.

She nodded, already missing his presence. But only because he'd saved her life. Not for anything else. Maybe if she lied to herself enough, she'd start to believe it.

"Jesus, Mari. What's going on? I drove by your place and this looks targeted. None of your neighbors' houses were hit. Whoever did this shot at your place, turned around at the end of the cul-de-sac, then came back and shot it up some more on their way out."

"How does my place look?" She didn't even want to think about the damage. Was enraged and terrified that her sanctuary had been violated.

"That's not important. What's going on?"

"I'm not totally sure."

"But you have an idea?"

"Yeah, maybe," she said on a sigh, then froze when Jeremy Ackerman's name popped up on her caller ID. "Hold that thought." She debated not answering, but on the third ring, picked up. "Mr. Ackerman." Unlike most of her clients, he hadn't told her to call him Jeremy and instead seemed to prefer a more formal address.

He cleared his throat. "Ms. Kim." She'd told him to call her Mari, but he was sticking to the whole formal thing.

"How can I help you?" They weren't supposed to fly until next week.

"I need a last-minute pilot for a trip to north Florida. Right past Destin, so not too far."

"When?"

"Today. In the next couple hours."

"Unfortunately I've already got a job lined up," she lied. She wasn't going to give him any personal details, especially since she wasn't sure that he wasn't involved with the shooting.

"Well that is unfortunate." His voice didn't change one iota in inflection. "Since we're still in the temporary stage I think I should tell you that I don't think our business relationship is going to work out. Gary talks so highly of you, but I need someone who is readily available."

She gritted her teeth, biting back a retort about his shady dealings nearly getting her killed today. She wasn't sure it had anything to do with him. Not a hundred percent. And there was no sense in tipping him off that she suspected him. "It sounds like we have different expectations, and we all need to be happy with who we work with. My assistant will send you a final bill."

"Thank you."

After a few more short pleasantries, she ended the call.

"Whoa."

She looked up at Bradford's voice. "What?"

"I've never heard that Mari before."

"I was perfectly pleasant!"

"Yeah, for a robot. I mean, you sounded super professional, but I like the real Mari better."

She snickered slightly, then straightened when Colin stepped back into the room. "Ackerman just called me." She was hugely relieved that their dealings were finished and she wouldn't have to see him again.

His eyes widened as she relayed the conversation. Then she recapped everything that had happened the day before with Ackerman to Bradford so he was up to speed.

"So this guy, is he somehow involved with whatever happened?" Bradford asked.

"I don't know. Nothing about today makes sense. It seems like such an escalation from me hearing a heated conversation to shooting up my place. We're lucky we weren't killed," she said.

"Maybe."

"What do you mean, maybe?" She frowned at Bradford.

"I only drove by your place, but all the bullet holes were in the top part of your house. Along the eaves and gutters. I think maybe one window was damaged, but it almost seemed like they were trying to miss. Don't get me wrong, your place—or you—were clearly targeted, but they might have just been trying to scare you."

Colin nodded in agreement.

Groaning, she laid her head down on the table and wished for this nonsense to be over. "What the hell is going on?"

"We'll figure it out," Bradford said. "Until then, you're staying with one of us. Magnolia's already said—"

"She'll be staying with me." There was no room for argument in Colin's deep voice.

She sat up, blinked at him. "What?"

"We don't have a connection—other than through your brother. And everyone knows how you feel about me. It makes more sense for you to stay with me."

She refused to feel guilty for disliking him. He deserved it. But she had to admit that what he'd done today made her dislike him a whole lot less. "You were seen with me today."

He gritted his teeth, and even though she could see he wanted to argue with her, he bit back whatever he was about to say.

"I think the two of you should lie low somewhere together," Bradford interjected.

"Agreed," Colin said immediately.

She narrowed her gaze at him. "You're surprisingly okay with this."

"I'm not okay with any of this, but I'm not letting you out of my sight." There was a whole lot of determination in his words. And maybe some heat.

Or maybe she was just projecting. But before she could analyze his tone, Camila finally walked in the door.

CHAPTER 8

"We should head over there now," Magnolia said as she secured the glass container full of lasagna she'd finished making for Mari.

"They're still getting settled in." Bradford kept his tone mild. Magnolia was Mari's best friend, but it had been clear there was something going on with Mari and Colin. Soooo he wanted to see how it played out, because Mari deserved happiness. Even if she was too stubborn to admit that there was a spark between her and Colin. "And that Colin guy is clearly capable."

Magnolia just snorted in annoyance and grumbled something under her breath.

"He saved her life." Bradford looked up as Ezra stepped into the room.

"Babe, why don't you relax and I'll pack all this up?" Ezra kissed her soundly, his hand cupping her slightly protruding stomach as he pulled her close.

Bradford looked away from them, wanting to give them privacy, even though he was glad for one of his best friends. He'd never seen Ezra this happy, hadn't even known it was possible for the guy to smile so much.

"I'll be waiting in the car for you two," Magnolia said as she stepped back, her words as strained as her expression.

"Everything okay?" Bradford asked once it was just him and Ezra.

His friend glanced over his shoulder, likely to make sure Magnolia was out of earshot of the kitchen. Once the front door shut and closed, he nodded. "She's just wound up about Lucas."

Their oldest son.

"Why?"

"Just college stuff. And I think some of it is pregnancy hormones." He basically whispered the last part.

"Not that you'd ever say that out loud, right?" Jesus, even Bradford knew better than that.

"Hell no. She's just worried about Lucas making the right decision about his future and now she's really worried about Mari. Today's been a lot."

"Yeah, I get that. But Berlin is doing her thing. She'll figure out what's going on with Mari." Their favorite hacker was digging into whoever this Jeremy Ackerman was as they spoke.

And that guy was screwed if he was behind the attack on Mari. Because all of them at Redemption Harbor Security would take him down.

Mari might not officially work with them, but she was one of them. Magnolia loved her like she was family, and Mari had dropped what she was doing more than once to fly them into places when they needed an extra pilot. Usually when Adalyn was off on a job.

"All things Magnolia's aware of. But..." Ezra shrugged.

"Mari's her best friend." Bradford understood. He'd do anything for his friends. People who'd become more family than anything over the last few years.

"Exactly." Ezra finished putting the rest of the containers into the oversized insulated bag. "And now the two of them are going to have enough food for at least a week."

"Did Magnolia make any extra lasagna?" He glanced in the refrigerator, making Ezra laugh.

"Yes, and we'll eat once we drop this off. Now come on. Pretty sure Magnolia will leave us if we don't hurry."

***

Mari leaned her head on Magnolia's shoulder as they kicked their feet up on the coffee table in the safe house. "I can't wait until this little person starts kicking." She rested her hand on her best friend's little baby bump.

Magnolia set her hand over hers. "You just have to be around for that to happen."

Mari's head popped up at the sound of tears in her friend's voice. It was just the two of them, since Magnolia had kicked out Ezra, Bradford and Colin not too long after they'd arrived at the two-story safe house she was currently relegated to. "Hey, don't cry."

"I can't help it." Magnolia wiped at her cheeks. "I've been a mess the last few weeks, and oh my god, you got shot at. I swear I'm not trying to make it about me."

"Stop with that. It can be about you today and every day. I'm fine. Everything is fine. And you know Berlin will figure out what's going on."

"Yeah, probably." She blinked away the last of her tears. "But Lucas is talking about moving out next year and...I'm not ready for this!"

She took Magnolia's hand and squeezed. "I can only imagine. But...it sounds like he might be staying close to home?"

"I'm just worried that he's staying in New Orleans because of his girlfriend."

"I thought you liked her?" Emma was as cute as a button, and sure they were young, but so what? The girl was smart as hell, kind and had a good head on her shoulders.

"Oh, I do. She's wonderful, but I just don't want him to limit himself. I don't want him to be afraid to spread his wings. I don't...want him making any mistakes."

Mari snorted. "He's human so the mistake thing is happening. And you've raised an incredibly smart—and emotionally mature—son. That boy is way more mature than we were at his age."

Magnolia laughed lightly. "No kidding. But we grew up pretty fast." Her tone sobered and Mari could only imagine what she was thinking.

"You got pregnant at a young age and people said you'd made a mistake. That you'd lost out on a good future. And now look at you. You've got a thriving business and you're helping all sorts of people start fresh. Not to mention you're a kickass mom. There isn't one right path for everyone. You've literally done what a good parent is supposed to do—you gave him all the tools and now he's got to start making these big future decisions for himself. And seriously, how can you be sad he might stay local?"

Magnolia swiped at a few stray tears. "How do you always know the right thing to say?"

"It's my best friend superpower."

"God, I love you." She laid her head against Mari's and sighed. "And I know you're right. I'm not-so-secretly glad he's staying. I guess I just feel a little selfish being so happy and...these hormones are no joke."

"I bet Ezra's happy Lucas is staying too. They've really bonded the last few months." And Mari loved seeing it. The two of them were so similar and both incredibly protective of Magnolia. When this new nugget arrived, watch out.

"I know. That's been the biggest relief. They're so much alike and I swear they gang up on me."

"Gang up on you? Like, they both tell you to put your feet up and take it easy?"

Magnolia nudged her thigh. "Don't you start too."

"Well you *are* having a geriatric pregnancy."

Magnolia snort-laughed. "Whoever came up with that term needs a good punch in the throat."

Mari snickered. "Right?"

"So...you okay staying here with Colin?" Magnolia asked, glancing toward the entryway.

The guys were all in the kitchen and out of earshot.

"Yeah." Mari didn't want to get into anything, especially her weird feelings for him. "He saved my life."

"I guess he's got that going for him," Magnolia grumbled.

"Look, what he said was years ago. I'm letting it go." And she meant it. "Pretty sure today negates everything."

Saving her life was definitely a big deal. Now she needed to move past her stupid feelings for him. Because it didn't matter that she was letting the past go, she flat-out couldn't be attracted to him.

She just couldn't.

CHAPTER 9

The ONLY time you have too much fuel is when you're on fire.

"You've got good friends," Colin murmured as they sat at the kitchen table, plates of lasagna in front of them.

"I really do." Mari had finally convinced Magnolia that she could leave, and now they were diving into some of the food they'd left behind. It was only a little awkward being under one roof with him, mainly because he was being sweet and he'd saved her life today. So she was feeling vulnerable and...a little attracted to him. But just because he'd saved her, that was all. It had nothing to do with the way his T-shirt molded to his biceps and chest, revealing just how fit the man was.

At least the place was relatively large so she could hibernate in another room if things got too weird.

"Though I am curious why they have a safe house at all."

She shrugged in what she hoped was a nonchalant manner. "Sometimes their clients need to lie low. Usually domestic violence situations."

He raised an eyebrow, but nodded. "That makes sense."

It was true, even if it wasn't the only reason they had multiple safe houses in the city and beyond.

"So, you and Bradford ever date?"

She paused with her fork halfway to her mouth, the tantalizing scent of all the cheese and pasta filling the air. "Uh, what?"

Colin shrugged, but there was nothing casual about his question. "Just curious. You seemed very comfortable together."

"We're friends. And not that it's any of your business, but no. He's just fun to hang out with." She didn't understand why he even cared if she'd dated Bradford. Sure, she was having thoughts about Colin that involved him in various states of undress, but there was no way he was having the same ones about her. She knew where she stood with him—she was Evan's little sister, end of story.

"Magnolia seems happy with Ezra," he said, thankfully changing the subject. "Though I'm pretty sure she still doesn't like me."

"She's incredibly happy. And I'm sure my brother told you the whole story about why they were separated?" Mari decided to ignore the last bit, because it was definitely true. Magnolia didn't hold grudges like Mari did, but they were best friends, so if *she* didn't like someone, Magnolia didn't like them.

He nodded, his expression darkening. "Yeah."

"So she deserves happiness more than anyone."

He nodded in agreement. "Are you ever going to tell me what happened between us? Why one day you just decided that you hated me?"

"I really just want to eat dinner and crash." It had been a ridiculously long day for both of them. "And I really want to play the 'I got shot at' card, but you did too."

He simply raised an eyebrow in response.

And fine, he *had* saved her life. Ugh, fine, they were apparently doing this now. She set her fork down, eyeing him across the table. Might as well get this over with now. If she was truly going to put this behind her, this was a necessary step. "When I was seventeen, I overheard you tell Grayson Sutton that I had an STI and that if he valued his genitalia, he'd stay away from me."

Colin blinked once. Twice. Went a little pale. "Oh...*Shit*. I *did* say that."

"Yep." She picked her fork back up, scooped up some creamy goodness—Magnolia made it with cheese substitutes for her because she was a goddess. Though at this point her stomach had twisted into a tight knot regardless. But she was exhausted and knew she'd sleep better if she ate. And she wasn't going to run out of here anyway. Nope, not happening. She would finish this conversation like an adult. *Double ugh.* Being an adult sucked. And it wasn't like she'd done anything wrong so she wasn't leaving all this food.

He scrubbed a hand over his face and sat back in the chair. The kitchen was large and looked like it hadn't been updated since the nineties, but it was cozy and right now the only sound was the icemaker in the refrigerator, churning out ice. "I'm not making excuses, but for context, he was a pig. He wanted to ask you out, so I lied to him to scare him off. I was young and stupid and was trying to keep him away from you."

"You weren't that young." He'd been home on leave, was well out of school—he'd been old enough to know better.

"I know. It was messed up. I was trying to look out for you but I didn't stop to think how it would affect you, and I'm sorry."

"Why did you even care if he asked me out?"

"He screwed anything that moved."

"And you just assumed I'd go out with him?"

Colin was still leaning back, not touching his food. "Yeah. He was...conventionally attractive. I don't think anyone ever said no to him."

"And you thought I...what, didn't know about his reputation? Or couldn't make the decision for myself?"

His jaw tightened. "He wasn't good enough for you, so I lied. For the record, I later told him that I'd lied and that he better stay away from you regardless."

"Why?" It made no sense why he'd felt the need to protect her like that. She got that he was best friends with her brother, but she could take care of herself.

"For all the reasons I've said. He wasn't good enough for you."

"You don't even *sound* sorry now."

"I'm sorry for lying about you. *That* I'm sorry for. But...I'm not sorry for warning that asshole off."

He seemed sincere. "I don't even know what to say to that."

Colin shrugged in that maddening way of his and she didn't know if she wanted to punch or kiss him.

Or both. And she was not in the right headspace for this nonsense. She'd almost been shot dead today. It had to be the reason for all these feelings bubbling up inside her. "Fine. I accept your half-assed apology, but only because you saved my life today. So now we're even."

He gave her a small grin, his mouth curving up in the sexiest way and she knew she was in trouble where he was concerned. "So we're friends now?"

"I wouldn't go that far."

"Well, we're stuck under the same roof for now."

"For one night only. Tomorrow we'll figure something else out." Because this wasn't a long-term solution. She had a job to do, contracts to honor—a professional reputation she'd worked hard to cultivate. She wasn't letting it vanish because of this nonsense.

And she knew that if she was alone with Colin for much longer while feeling so off-kilter, she was at risk of making a stupid decision and giving in to her attraction to him. Which would be bad for two reasons. One, he would be into it and then they'd both regret it afterward. Or two, he would reject her and she would never live down the humiliation.

CHAPTER 10

A good landing is one you can walk away from. A great landing is when you can use the plane again.

"It's going to be fine," Mari said into her phone as she poured a mug of coffee, inhaling the rich scent. She wasn't sure who she was trying to convince more, herself or Berlin.

"You can't be sure. But if you stay where you are, then you're ninety-nine percent more likely to be safe," Berlin said.

"Did you just pull that statistic right out of your butt?"

"I have a great butt."

"I know and, oh my god, we're getting off topic." She pulled open the fridge, grinned at the array of flavored creamer inside. The Redemption Harbor crew had really stocked this place up for her.

Colin walked into the kitchen then—shirtless.

Yes, shirtless. She felt it bore repeating because oh. My. God. She hadn't had coffee and wasn't even sure there was enough coffee in the world for this.

It was like he'd walked right off the set of an action movie with ripped abs and... Wait, Berlin had said something. "What?" she managed to get out and was glad that Colin was looking longingly at the coffee pot and not noticing her drool over him. See? This right here was why she had to get the hell out of there.

"I asked what your pilot friend has to say about it."

"He's fine with it. Totally on board. I've gotta go." She hung up, then turned down her ringer.

But three texts popped up one after the other.

Liar!

We've got people sitting on your place and his. We have this under control.

Do NOT go anywhere. OR ELSE.

Jeez, how did Berlin text so fast? Setting her phone down, she poured creamer into her mug as Colin leaned against the countertop, coffee mug in hand.

"So what am I on board with...if you were referring to me?"

"Ah, I was. So Gary called this morning and needs me for a last-minute flight to pick him up."

"Nope."

She arched an eyebrow at him. "Well, I wasn't asking."

"You can't go anywhere right now."

"Being in the air is the safest place to be." She didn't have a death wish. And besides, she was right. While flying, she'd be safe and far away from here. "If anything, I'll be even safer than here on the ground where anyone could walk through that door and...bam!" Unlikely, since no one knew their location and the Redemption Harbor crew had been careful. But she could be theatrical at times.

He looked as if his head was about to explode, but to her surprise, he took a sip of his coffee and calmly said, "What if one of my guys picked him up?"

"I could ask, but he's prickly and doesn't like change. It's an OCD thing—as in diagnosed. He's very particular. And before you ask, there's no way he'd let anyone else fly his plane. I don't think his insurance would be okay with it anyway. I'm the only one contracted."

Colin was silent for a long moment and she had to actively not stare at his bare chest. Seriously, why wasn't he wearing a shirt? Was he messing with her? Or was this how he just normally walked around? Clearly it had been too long since she'd gotten naked with anyone. Combine that with how raw she was feeling—it was the only thing to explain this attraction. And it would go away, she was sure of it.

"Look, he's my oldest client, Colin. I need his business." She didn't need Colin's permission or anything, but she wanted him to understand why this was so important to her. He was a small business owner now too.

Sighing, he finally nodded. "Fine. I'll go get dressed."

"What? Why?"

"I'll drive you to the airport. I assume you've already checked the weather, but you can get started on filing your flight plan."

Oh. Well that was nice. "Ah, okay, thanks. I'll go change too." Because she was still in her pajamas. "I need to call Berlin back too before she sends over a SWAT team."

Colin just grinned and headed out and up the stairs. She tried not to stare, failed. Instead, she drank in the muscles along his spine, over his shoulders, imagined dragging her fingers along all that taut skin, and whew, he was out of sight.

Now she could breathe again. That man should not be allowed to just run around half dressed.

***

"So why does your client need you so last-minute? Is this normal?" Colin's tone was neutral enough, but she knew he was unhappy.

At least he wasn't arguing with her about this anymore. She didn't glance up from her tablet as she said, "It's very normal. And he's a political consultant. I'm not sure of all the specifics, but he travels a lot in the state and the immediate surrounding ones. Someone who hired him flew him up to Arkansas for a couple days, but from the sounds of it their dealings went sour and he's done. He wants to be gone yesterday. And he's paying me extra," she murmured as she finished up with her flight plan.

"What did Berlin say when you called her back?" He pulled into the airport parking lot.

"Ah, she was annoyed but agreed that I'd be safest flying. She also made it clear that she's tracking my phone, even though I gave her access to my flight." Mari laughed lightly.

"She sounds like a good friend."

"She is. Everyone at Redemption Harbor is." And Mari was grateful they were in her life. "Thanks for the ride. I also told Berlin that you would be heading directly back to the safe house, so don't make a liar out of me. I'll call you as soon as I—"

"Oh, I'm going with you. There's more than enough room for me and I'm sure your client will understand if he's really a good guy. I loaded up my backpack when you were getting dressed."

So clearly he'd been planning this. No wonder he hadn't argued with her. Sneaky, sneaky. She took a deep breath, dug down for calm. "Colin—"

But he was already out of the vehicle. *Damn it!* She grabbed her stuff and before she could get out, he'd already opened the door.

"Colin—"

"Feel free to keep saying my name, but either way I'm going. And it won't take you long to change the weight and balance so don't even start.

If I have to play the 'I saved your life so you owe me' card, I absolutely will."

"Oh. My. God. You can't just use that anytime you want something."

"I can when your life is literally in potential danger. And if you push back, I'll call your mother. Not your brother—your mom. Oh yeah, that's the real card I'm pulling."

That stopped her. "You wouldn't."

He showed her his cell phone and already had her mom's number pulled up. An adorable picture of the two of them was the image for her contact information.

"When did you take a selfie with my mom?" she grumbled, already grudgingly accepting that she'd lost this one.

"This was at a Christmas party two years ago."

She sniffed slightly. "Okay, fine. You can fly with me, *silently*. No side seat flying."

"Like totally silent, or can I tell you if I see some weird shit on radar?"

Sighing, she walked away from him even as she fought a smile. She'd forgotten how much she used to just plain like him. And right now she couldn't have any distractions.

Neither of them could.

Once she'd completed the preflight check and gotten her departure clearance from ATC, she could feel that sense of freedom once they hit three thousand feet AGL. She wasn't sure why, but she could finally take in a full, clear breath now that they were nearing cruising altitude.

"Maybe you weren't wrong about flying," Colin said over the headsets.

"Maybe? Come on. It's a gorgeous day and no one knows we're up here." Except the people they'd seen at the hangar and ATC, but whatever.

"I could get used to flying in this. It's like being in a luxury car."

"Right?" It was one of her favorite planes to fly. The designers had clearly had luxury in mind with plenty of legroom for passengers, buttery leather seats, and she loved the panoramic windows. Other than this she mostly flew Cessnas, which she liked, but the Cirrus was still a favorite.

"What about your client?" Colin continued. "Would he say anything to Ackerman about you flying today?"

"I don't think so. I told him I needed to talk to him about something related to Ackerman when I picked him up today. He texted back that it was fine and that he's not really friends with the guy anyway. More like associates. Sounds like he met him through one of his political contacts. I don't think he'd say anything to him... I can't imagine they talk about me at all." But maybe she should have been more specific. She shook her head lightly. "So how's your job been going anyway? Since you got out of the Air Force?" Now that they'd cleared the air, she found that she liked being around him. Even if she found him ridiculously attractive—to the point of distraction. She wasn't sure if he felt the same way. He was too hard to read, and his whole overprotective vibe was pretty much standard so that didn't help at all.

"Well when a certain pilot isn't trying to steal my clients—"

"You stole my client first."

"You swiped land that I'd all but bought."

"If you want to get technical. But I'd say we're even at this point." She grinned at him before looking back out the dash. "Look, I'll sell you that land for what I bought it for."

"Seriously?"

She shrugged as she eyed the dash, spotted a couple planes on the TAS well below them as they increased to a slightly higher cruising speed. "Yeah, I don't need it. I mean, I could use it. And whatever, you saved my life. So if I do this, then you can't play that card again."

"Hmm, I might not want to buy it then, because I intend to play this card for yeaaars."

She shook her head, but then straightened when the panels on the dash went dark.

The plane dropped slightly and her stomach went along with it. But panicking was the last thing she could do.

Colin straightened next to her as well, but it was clear that something was wrong as everything went silent, the propellor completely dying. They'd lost power.

Even though she knew them by heart, she pulled out the short checklist of emergency procedures while still steering the plane. She tried to restart the engine, but it was completely dead. Even though her heart rate kicked up, she'd been in this situation more than once and knew not to panic. Planes didn't just fall out of the sky without power—though this wouldn't be as smooth as if she'd been flying a sport plane, those babies floated no matter what.

She could land this—she just had to be calm. And if she couldn't handle gliding it to a landing, she could activate the parachute.

"The field to the northeast of us is a good candidate for landing," Colin said, his tone even.

"I agree." They were near St. Francisville, an area she'd flown over many times before. There were a lot of green open areas interspersed throughout the forests.

Damn it.

The familiarity of the area made this easier and so did his presence. And thankfully Colin was stone-cold relaxed, not that she'd expect any less. "Nearest airport is False River, but you're right, that field is our best shot." They weren't going to make it any farther. "Wind's out of the south, determining best glide speed," she said, even though Colin knew what she was doing. But it was easier to talk herself through an emergency landing. It helped keep her mind on her tasks and not on the fact that they'd lost power completely.

After determining the glide speed and trimming the plane, she squawked 7700 on the transponder, indicating an emergency situation.

Looking at her emergency checklist, she started getting into the pattern, treating the field exactly like she would a runway. Landing in one piece was the priority.

As they hit a bump of turbulence, she eyed nearby power lines and two towers, thankfully well out of the way. She visually scanned below them and determined that the grassy field was still the best place to land.

She reached up, skimmed her fingers over the red handle that would deploy the CAPS parachute system should they need it. It made her feel better knowing it was there, but she didn't think they'd need it.

As she flew, Colin changed the dial to the emergency guard channel 121.5 "Mayday, mayday, Cirrus..."

He gave their call sign and location as she established the 1,000 feet AGL and was abeam the imaginary touchdown point as she continued to glide the plane into the base leg.

"I'm getting nothing," he said through the headset, though she'd heard the same.

Or rather *hadn't* heard a response. They were on their own.

As she abeamed the point, she didn't have to cut the power like she normally would have because they had none, then she put the nose down as she made the turn.

"Approaching final, unlatch doors," she said as they began the final descent. The familiar repetition was more for herself than anything else. She was trying to treat this like a normal landing when it was anything but.

He opened his door at the same time that she popped hers open. In an emergency, the last thing you wanted was to end up trapped so it made sense to open the doors before landing. So far, this was relatively smooth—emergency landings were rarely like in the movies where planes just dropped from the sky. That wasn't how it happened as long as the pilot kept the plane's nose down and maintained the best glide speed. And you know, didn't run into any power lines or ridiculous windshear while landing. The important thing really was to stay calm.

As she neared their makeshift runway, she slightly pulled the nose up and breathed out a sigh of relief once she felt the upward flare, then touchdown.

They rumbled along, the field bumpier than she'd realized, the plane still shuddering, but the grass slowed the plane down a lot faster than a paved runway.

Once they came to a full stop, she slid her headset off and unstrapped as relief punched through her. She got out at the same time Colin did, but she reached into the back seat for a tool kit. "I'm going to unscrew the cowling, see what the hell is going on." Because they should never have lost full power. She'd filed a flight plan, so it wasn't like they were missing. Sooner or later when she didn't close out said plan, someone would figure out something had gone wrong.

But they were miles from actual civilization, which meant if they couldn't get this plane started, they were going to have to hoof it out of here.

"What the hell?" After lifting off the cowling, she stared down at the fried engine. Two of the computer components looked as if they'd been torched.

"I've seen this before," Colin muttered before he reached down into the open engine and pulled out a small magnetic device. "It's a remote EMP." An electromagnetic pulse.

She blinked, but plucked it from his hand to inspect it. "Wait...what? I thought planes were shielded against EMP strikes or attacks." It was how they were built, for very obvious reasons.

"From lightning and solar flare types of EMP strikes, yes. And combat aircraft have a different type of shield altogether...which is not important. This type of plane does have shielding, but not from someone planting this." He took it back, inspected it carefully. "This is along the lines of a military-grade weapon."

A shiver rolled down her spine as the implication of what had happened settled in her bones. "So someone tried to kill us. Again." They had a parachute but now she was wondering if that had been tampered with too.

Colin nodded, his expression dark as he scanned the skies. "And we need to get out of here because pretty soon whoever did this will realize they failed. They likely thought killing the electronics would cause a crash immediately."

Which meant they didn't know much about planes. Thankfully.

With trembling hands, she grabbed the backpack she brought with her on every flight and Colin pulled out his own small one. Every pilot she knew brought a small bag even for short flights, with water and snacks.

Because you never knew what could happen.

"How's your phone looking?" she asked as they headed for the nearby tree line. "Because I have no service."

"Me neither." His expression was grim. "But I do have a compass. We need to head northwest. Let's get moving."

Freaking fantastic.

CHAPTER 11

It's always a good idea to keep the pointy end going forward as much as possible.

"Come on." Mari growled down at her phone in clear frustration.

"We'll get service eventually." Colin's phone didn't have service either, but they'd deal with it. "I've hiked in Tunica Hills before and sometimes I'll get service but mostly I don't. It's this general area, I think."

She still grumbled but tucked her phone into her backpack. "Hopefully someone will be able to track the plane."

The National Transportation Safety Board would likely work with locals—state troopers or a nearby sheriff's department, it just depended. But they needed to get out of here regardless. "We should be gone before that happens." Under different circumstances, he might have stayed nearby, but the plane had been sabotaged. And at this point they had to assume it was Ackerman. Her client could have easily told him about this morning's flight. Not to mention anyone at the hangar.

It hadn't been empty when they'd been there. There'd been at least a dozen different people milling about.

Though she'd been scheduled to fly the plane tomorrow anyway, so the EMP could have been planted at any time in preparation for her next flight.

Which meant they had no idea who had done it. Not without getting a look at the camera feeds at the hangar, and even then... He sighed, shelving those thoughts.

Right now his priority was getting them to safety. Mari was more than capable, but he was the one with the survival training. Not that he thought they'd need it for what was essentially a long-ass hike through the forest. But he was still glad for the training. And at least it was still early enough that they had plenty of daylight and the real summer wasn't here yet so it wasn't sweltering. "You hear that?" he murmured as he paused by the tree line, taking in the quiet.

From the map and what he'd seen aerially, there was at least six hundred acres of green surrounding them. He'd seen a few farmhouses dotted below before they'd landed, and a property he recognized as a horse farm. That was the closest, so heading there was the plan.

"It's like a buzzing—"

"It's a drone. More than one. Shit. Come on." The back of his neck tingled as they hurried deeper into the forest. They were close to a national park—one that didn't see much foot traffic.

"Drones?" Mari whispered. "That's weird, right?"

He nodded. "Especially with your plane being sabotaged. And now random drones show up? Could be someone local but..."

"Let's see if we can spot them before they spot us?" She had the straps of her backpack cinched around her chest and waist and her dark hair pulled up into a short ponytail.

"Exactly. I'm not trying to give you orders, but it'll be better if you hunker down while I head back out there."

She nodded and glanced around before pointing at a huge gap in an old oak tree. "I'll hide in there." She was already moving, crawling through fallen brown leaves to hide among large, exposed roots.

As he hurried back to the tree line and the direction of where they'd left the plane, he could barely see her. And if he hadn't been looking for her, he wouldn't have known she was there.

That made it easier for him to leave her.

Because everything about this situation was bizarre. Her friend Berlin had done something to their phones and assured them that they weren't being tracked by anyone, so he didn't think they were at risk of being found that way. But it was something to consider.

The buzzing was louder now so he slowed, going down on one knee as he crouched behind the trunk of a southern live oak that had to be a few hundred years old. Keeping his backpack on, he pulled out his phone, turned on the video function and zoomed in as far as he could, then slowly slid it around the trunk.

The buzzing was louder now but he didn't hear voices.

Still, he wasn't taking any risks. He'd seen some next-gen tech while in the Air Force and wasn't going to underestimate whatever this was. After recording for about thirty seconds, he pulled his phone back to him.

The angle was awkward, but he watched as two small drones buzzed around the plane. One was smaller than the other, but they both seemed to be inspecting the plane from all angles.

Slowly, methodically.

He zoomed in on the video, trying to get a better look at what they were dealing with, but everything was grainy.

Suddenly the buzzing grew louder as if it was headed in his direction. He plastered himself back up against the tree.

Moments later, one of the drones zipped by, deeper into the forest.

He remained still, waiting to see if he'd been spotted. The machine looked as if it had a camera on the front, but he'd been trying to stay immobile and out of sight.

Taking a chance, he peered back around the tree and saw the other drone disappear past the tree line on the opposite side of the clearing.

Okay, so someone was definitely looking for them. And there was no way they were friendlies. Because the one thing he was sure of was that these weren't normal drones you could buy at a big-box store. This was some serious tech so he doubted the drones were being piloted by some random farmer who'd seen their plane.

Moving fast in the direction the drone had flown, he veered off slightly to the east so he didn't follow it exactly.

He was headed back to Mari, but didn't want to give away her location in case he was spotted. Unfortunately he couldn't even text her because he still didn't have service.

When he heard the buzz again, he lay flat against a fallen log. From his angle he couldn't see it, but the buzzing sound traveled back the way it had come.

Once it sounded far enough away, he rolled up and jumped over the log then sprinted back to Mari's hiding spot. "Hey," he whispered as he slid in between the roots with her.

"Did you see the drone? It came through here but didn't linger. Just flew through, then sort of looped back around. It looked like almost military grade."

"There are two of them, and whatever they are, they're not cheap. They inspected the plane then split up. They're looking for us."

Her jaw clenched tight. "Should we try to take them out?"

"I don't think so. I don't want them to see us at all if possible. That way they don't know which direction we went. And if they don't have any idea..." He trailed off at another buzzing sound.

Mari scooted back deeper into the shadows of the roots and he did the same, gathering some of the leaves and pulling them up over their sneakers and legs.

The drone flew up higher in the trees, making it difficult to see. But the buzzing remained. It drifted away momentarily, then grew louder, then drifted, and on and on as it continued scouring the woods.

An hour later it flew back in the direction it had originally come. After thirty minutes of silence, he said, "Want to stay?"

"It's been half an hour. I say we start making our way toward that horse farm. If the drones come back, we should hear them. And it's not like they can watch us from the sky. Not yet anyway."

At her words he looked up. The forest here was too thick for any eyes in the sky to see them well, if at all. And no matter what kind of tech they were, they would have to recharge eventually.

***

"Well, shit." Mari looked over the edge of washed-away road to the canyon below.

Yeah, Colin seconded that. "This wasn't on the map."

"I know." She looked up at him in surprise. "This wasn't your fault. I'm not, like, blaming you."

They'd been hiking the last two hours and were well into the afternoon, steadily making their way through mostly woods until they'd found the hiking path and then road they'd been looking for. Unfortunately there was a huge crater in the road, with a yawning clay canyon beneath it.

"This should be roped off or something though," she muttered, looking back down at it.

"It doesn't look like this area gets many visitors." There was a huge rock face next to the drop-off with plenty of space to walk around, and no graffiti. That was the giveaway for him. Because hikers and campers often couldn't resist leaving their mark and there was nothing on that rock.

"It almost feels like we're the last two people on earth." She shivered slightly. "It's weird."

"I know." He'd been in more remote places than this, but she wasn't wrong. "If it wasn't for the couple planes we saw overhead I'd feel like we were on another planet."

She nodded and looked back at the crumbling road. "Want to risk moving around this?" She motioned at the slim strip of asphalt still standing that would allow them to make their way around it to the other side.

"There's nothing to hold on to if we fall or if it breaks away beneath us." He looked past the rock face. "But we could try climbing around it, then coming down on the other side."

Mari looked at the briar-covered boulder dubiously.

"I'll boost you up."

"You just want to touch my butt," she muttered. Then her eyes widened as she looked at him. "Obviously I'm kidding."

"Well you're not wrong." What he wouldn't give to get his hands on her. But now was definitely not the time.

She stared at him. Blinked once. Twice. Then turned away from him. "Okay, then."

Damn it. Maaaaybe he should have kept his mouth shut. Before he could say anything, she swiveled. "Drone!"

And that was when he saw it, way across the canyon hovering above the pine trees of the forest—that would eventually lead them to semi-civilization.

It started in their direction.

"There's nowhere to hide," he muttered. "And I've seen drones that disperse weaponized biological agents. Doubtful that this drone has that capability." But he liked to keep shit like that in mind. Right now everything was a threat to Mari as far as he was concerned and his only job was to keep her safe.

"I say we knock it out of the sky if it gets too close." Mari bent down and pretended to tie her shoe. "Act casual and grab my flare gun out of my pack. Once it gets close, let's take it out."

Colin did as she said, keeping his body angled in front of her so that whoever was manning the thing wouldn't see what he was doing. "If there's one, there's at least another one."

"I know, but taking out one's better than nothing. Once we incapacitate this one, I say we hunker down somewhere."

He nodded and still hadn't turned. "How far away is it?"

"Fifty feet," she murmured as she stood. "Crossing the canyon opening now. And there's definitely a camera on it. At your five o'clock and moving in."

He half turned at the approach, the buzzing annoying but a good indicator of its location even if he hadn't had Mari telling him where it was.

As he zeroed in on it, the drone slowed as it neared them then hovered, clearly deciding not to get too close.

Too late.

He raised the weapon, aimed, fired.

The flare made a loud whooshing sound as it exploded from the barrel then slammed right into the two-foot drone.

Metal and plastic splintered out in every direction. On instinct, he turned, using his body to cover Mari as parts hit his backpack and the backs of his legs.

"Colin!" she cried out and it took him a moment to realize she was worried about him, not hit.

"Are you okay?"

"Yeah, I'm fine. Are you?" she demanded, inspecting him as he took a small step back.

"I'm good." Glancing down into the open hole, he paused then looked at her. "Want to climb around or risk it?"

"Let's climb it and then regroup. I don't know if we should head to the horse farm anymore."

"I was thinking the same thing." It was the closest place according to the map. Exactly where their pursuers would expect them to go.

CHAPTER 12

Bradford looked at the screen Berlin had pulled up. The little dot that represented Mari was flickering out again. "At least she's been moving," he murmured, even though he was still worried.

It was just Berlin and Bradford at the office downtown, but the others were waiting for their report. Bradford knew he didn't have to be here, but he wanted to be close by, so he had updates as soon as they came in.

Berlin had discovered that Mari hadn't closed out her flight plan and was basically MIA. Bradford was still learning about all this flight stuff, but it was his understanding that Mari had requested a "flight following" as she usually did when taking routine flights. Her route had ended in the middle of a field partway to her destination. The plane she was flying was equipped with ADS-B, a nav system that tracked aircraft in real time. So at least they knew where the plane was and that it hadn't crashed.

"Yeah." But Berlin looked just as worried as him. She shoved up from her computer and stretched. "The Flight Service Station has issued an alert notice and now a search and rescue team has started looking for her and Colin, *officially*. But I still don't like this. That's a lot of landscape to cover and they're on foot. Or I'm assuming they are. The dispatched helicopters might not see them or even be able to get them out of there, depending on the terrain. And they don't know which direction they went."

"At least the authorities are taking this seriously." Words he was repeating to himself, though they weren't doing much to ease his worry. He adored Mari; they all did.

"I know. I just wish we could do more."

"Me too." Bradford's gaze strayed back to the second screen, eyeing the weather. "But Adalyn says she can't fly in this." Which he'd known, given the storms that had moved in from the west and were now covering the northwest part of Louisiana. "If we don't have anything pressing, I might drive up to St. Francisville, grab a room somewhere."

"There's not much there. I've looked." Berlin glanced back at the screen with the weather radar. "But...I don't hate that idea. Rowan and Tiago are due back by Wednesday and they haven't needed me the last couple days. Chance and I could head out with you, just to be nearby

in case I find them and they need us."

Bradford nodded. "I think Ezra needs to stay close to home right now, even if he hasn't said anything."

"Agreed. Magnolia needs him even if she doesn't realize it. And they deserve the time together now. The three of us can handle this."

Ezra had missed her first pregnancy due to extenuating circumstances, and Bradford wanted his best friend to be there for everything this time. He'd lost so much time with the woman he loved. Bradford knew from personal experience how hard it was to lose someone, to not know where they were and why they'd ghosted you. "I'll text him, ask him to be our backup with Adalyn in case we need them."

"Sounds good to me. I'll let Chance know to pack up and we can head out soon."

Bradford just hoped that they found Mari and Colin. From what he knew of the other man, he had a decent amount of outdoor experience and had been a pilot for a little longer than Mari. The two of them were smart, but something must have happened for them to land the plane in the middle of nowhere.

And whatever that reason was, it wasn't a good one.

CHAPTER 13

"Are you freaking kidding me?" Mari wanted to cry. It was late afternoon, with sunset coming up faster than she wanted to think about.

They were still ten miles from the B&B they were sloooowly trekking toward.

A few raindrops had splattered against their faces over the last mile. She'd been hoping the storm would hold off, but as thunder rumbled overhead, the ground shaking with it, she knew that rain was coming.

"Here, help me with this." Colin crouched in front of his backpack and pulled out a dark green square.

"Is that a tarp?" Oh, please let it be one. She'd packed protein essentials, water, the flare gun, and extra clothes, like she always did for day trips. Clearly she needed to add more to her pack.

"Yep." He started to unfold it, so she grabbed the other end and worked with him until it was completely stretched out. "It's about eight by twelve feet."

"This thing is awesome. Did you get this in the military?"

He snorted as he pulled out paracord. "I actually found this at a home goods store when buying umbrellas for my back patio and snagged it. It's supposed to be used to keep out rain or snow on patios, and it's insulated and thick. I thought it would be perfect for camping."

"And it already has the holes for hanging. I might get one of these, though I hope to never need it again."

"Right," he muttered as they started stringing it up between two trees.

As if on cue, the sky decided to open up with a clap of thunder. Rain soaked them as they continued working, but it didn't take more than a couple minutes to finish securing the four corners of the tarp.

Drenched through to her bones, she huddled under the tarp next to Colin, glad her pack wasn't totally soaked. Aaand, also glad that she was with Colin, for more reasons than she wanted to admit even to herself.

He wrapped an arm around her and held her close. Even though it wasn't that cold, the rain and wind added to the chill already permeating her thanks to all her clothes being wet.

"At least an ALNOT should have been issued by now." Once the alert notice went out that she hadn't closed out her flight plan or arrived at her destination, things would start moving. Hopefully they already had. She curled up against him, trying to get warmer. Her teeth chattered as rain pounded down around their makeshift cover. Colin was so big and solid. She pressed closer, grateful for the heat of his body, wondered if it would be inappropriate to ask him to take off his shirt so she could get extra warmth.

Hmm, yep, it would, but the thought was tempting.

So far the tarp was holding under the onslaught of rain. But the forested hillside they were on was quickly gathering little streams of water—and mud.

So that was going to be fun to trek through later.

For now she chose to ignore it because there was nothing either one of them could do about it. They had ten more miles to go before they reached shelter, something she had to keep repeating to herself.

"Yeah, I'm hoping that chopper we heard earlier was search and rescue," Colin said.

"Hopefully it'll scare off the drones too. What a mess." Her teeth still chattered, though that was partially from her growing anger at the whole situation.

At *Ackerman*, if he was indeed behind this. And she couldn't see how he wasn't at this point. The conversation she'd overheard in the hangar hadn't even been that bad. Not great, but now someone had tried to kill her.

Twice.

"I'm sorry you got dragged into this with me," she continued. For that alone she wanted to take down Ackerman.

"I'm not."

She looked up at him, and his blue eyes darkened slightly. "Seriously?"

He shrugged, that little grin pulling at the corners of his full lips. Seriously, why did a guy get a mouth like that? And ridiculously long eyelashes? Ugh. Not fair.

"So you like having to perform an emergency landing, then being stuck in the middle of the woods in a rainstorm while being chased by drones?"

"Sounds like a good time to me. Just another adventure." That tug was now a full grin, and sweet flying raptors, she wanted to kiss him.

At that thought, she stilled.

Apparently he read her mind, or maybe she was reading his, because he leaned down, taking her by complete surprise as he slanted his mouth over hers. And he moved slowly enough that she could pull back if she wanted. Could easily tell him to stop.

But the cold had clearly gone straight to her head because she met him halfway, sliding her hand over his chest, clutching onto his shoulder as he teased his tongue against hers in slow, sensual strokes.

Enjoying the playful way he kissed, she settled against him, feeling more relaxed than she had in years around him. Maybe it was because they were in the middle of nowhere, dependent on each other, but she wanted him more than she could remember ever wanting anyone. So she embraced this.

When he nipped her bottom lip, she moaned into his mouth and felt his entire body tense.

All his muscles tightened, and oh, she liked that. Liked that her simple moan had him reacting. Even though the alarm in her head that reminded her how stupid this was kept going off because she couldn't run out on him after their kiss, couldn't pretend it hadn't happened, she didn't pull back.

He tasted like the chocolate bar they'd shared earlier, sweet, and oh god, she loved the feel of his muscular chest under her fingertips. It had been ages since she'd been with anyone and right about now she was feeling touch starved. It was taking all her restraint not to climb on top of him, straddle him— They both pulled back at the same time at a crashing sound.

Alarm punching through her, she started to get up but stilled when Colin placed a warning hand on her thigh.

"Look."

She followed his gaze and saw two giant boars snorting and racing through the rain, slipping and sliding down a nearby hill.

She wasn't even sure why, but she laughed. "They look like big dogs having a good time."

He snickered next to her as one dove in a muddy pool about twenty yards away before it continued into the thick of trees. "Living their best life for sure."

Sighing, she laid her head against his shoulder and closed her eyes. "I say we just chalk this up to being stuck in the middle of nowhere." Because she didn't want to talk about the kiss. To hear him apologize or...whatever.

He tucked her close, his protective hold making her heart squeeze. "As soon as the rain clears, we'll head out. Or even if it just thins, I say we pack up and try to make it to that B&B before dark."

He hadn't responded to what she'd said, and she was happy to let it drop. "Works for me, because I do not want to camp out here overnight." Hell. No. That was when animals and other murder-y things came out.

Though... she didn't hate the idea of being cuddled up with him all night.

CHAPTER 14

Cranky when not flying.

"We're almost there," Colin said, urging Mari on. Darkness would be falling in the next hour and even though he would be fine sleeping in the woods, he didn't want that for her and it would be a lot easier for them if they found real shelter.

It would also give them a chance to call for help.

"You said that thirty minutes ago." Mari's damp hair was plastered to her face, her clothes soaked, her pants and boots covered in mud as she climbed over another fallen tree.

It really was like being at the end of the world out here. And she did *not* care for it.

"But I mean it this time. We're really close." He pointed in between two trees. "This way. See? This path is well worn."

She eyed the new pathway dubiously. "It's a muddy mess. And why are you so cheery?"

"I figure one of us needs to be."

"Normally it's me. I don't know what's wrong with me right now." She avoided a big puddle as the pathway widened a little more.

From the looks of it, he guessed it was a hiking path or maybe one for riding horses. "Nothing's wrong with you. You're dealing with a lot right now."

"You are too."

He shrugged. "Yeah, but I like being with you." He was sorry it had taken this for them to call a truce though.

"Now you're just making me feel bad," she muttered.

"Soooo are you saying you don't like being with me?" he teased.

"I don't love *this*...but I'm glad you're with me. It's a little scary to think how awful it would have been to do this alone. And then I feel guilty for being glad you're with me when some lunatic clearly wanted us to crash." She groaned slightly.

And all he could think about was that little moan from earlier. Something he was desperately trying not to think about at all. Not until he was in a very cold shower. Because she'd pulled back, had put up a very clear boundary. He wasn't going to talk to her about it, not now anyway. The priority was getting out of here. Getting her to safety.

Once that happened, his priorities would be a lot different.

He was at least getting her to talk to him, to open up. Because that kiss hadn't been a mistake, and he sure as hell wasn't going to chalk it up to them being out in the middle of nowhere.

He'd have kissed her in the middle of Jackson Square with a bunch of onlookers if she'd been willing. He'd kiss the gorgeous woman anywhere she wanted.

"People!" Mari put on a burst of speed as they reached a crossroads in the path and found a man in his fifties or sixties riding an older-looking horse.

And he was very surprised to see them. "Howdy," the man said.

Colin stepped up next to her, knowing what they looked like and hoping it worked in their favor because they needed a place to crash. "Hi. I'm Colin and this is Mari. We had an emergency and had to land our plane in the middle of a field. We've been hiking all day. Would you have a phone we could use? Or Wi-Fi?"

The man blinked down at them. "I heard about a search and rescue crew out today before the rain grounded them. Are you okay to walk or do you need to ride?" He looked at Mari. "Cuz I'll walk and you can ride Biscuit here." He gently patted the mare, who whinnied playfully in response.

"I'm okay, but thank you. We're just exhausted and really need to check in with the search and rescue team."

"All right, this way then. We're about a mile to the barn. Oh, my name's John Canfield. My wife is Becky," he said as he pulled out his cell phone. It was one of those clunky ones that were basically indestructible. "And it's no wonder your phones don't work out here. Only people who get service have the local phone carrier. But I'm letting my wife know to get a room set up for you. You're lucky... Well maybe that's the wrong word," he said with a grin, clearly a talker.

Which was fine with Colin. The guy was friendly and helping them—and he'd offered to let Mari ride his horse. Colin wished she'd taken him up on it, but understood why she'd said no.

"Either way we have two rooms currently available at our B&B. You can stay the night if you need to rest and freshen up. So what happened to your plane?"

Oh, they'd only be needing one room. He wasn't letting Mari out of his sight tonight.

"Technical issue," Mari said before Colin could think of an answer. "Luckily I always file a flight plan, but it was a heck of a place to have to land. We ran across a canyon where the road had washed away on our hike here."

"Oooh, boy. That's a dangerous area. Even the kids don't play around there anymore. One of our local teens broke a leg falling into the canyon and he's lucky that's all he broke." He shook his head. "I'm surprised y'all didn't stop at the Hanson's horse farm before making it here."

"I didn't see a horse farm on the map," Colin lied. "None of our electronics are working."

"Ah, yeah, our place has been here for decades so I'm not surprised it's on an actual map. Didn't know anyone used those anymore," he said with a chuckle as they neared the end of the pathway. "And here we are."

A woman with salt-and-pepper hair, wearing jeans and a button-down green and blue flannel shirt was waiting next to a barn.

In the distance beyond the barn was a white, columned antebellum mansion, and live oak trees that had to be hundreds of years old. There was also a string of little pastel-colored cottages in a sort of half circle around a giant pond. They looked modern compared to the mansion, had clearly been built on concrete slabs to withstand hurricanes and other Louisiana weather.

"Hey y'all, I've let the sheriff know you've been found. He's working with the search and rescue crew to find you both." She smiled warmly at them. "You look exhausted and I'm guessing you're hungry. One of our cottages is free if you'd like to clean up. You're actually just in time for dinner, so I can bring you a couple covered plates. Or if you want to join the others in the cafeteria I'm sure they'd love to talk to the people who crash-landed a plane."

"You are an angel," Mari said on a laugh, her smile making the other woman grin. "And luckily there was no crashing. Just gliding into a grassy field."

"That's probably a good thing," the woman said. "Oh, I'm Becky, by the way." She continued chatting as she led them away from the barn toward the cottages.

"Thank you so much for this," Colin said as she opened the door for them. "We're so grateful we found your place."

Becky waved her hand away at his thanks. "We're glad you two are safe. It's getting late, so unless you have a way to get out of here—and we're quite a ways from town—you can stay the night. On the house."

"Oh, we'll pay you—"

She shook her head. "Nope. I wouldn't hear of it. I'll be back in a bit with some food. There are clean towels in the bathroom."

"I'm so tempted to face-plant on the bed," Mari said as Colin locked the door behind them.

The cottage was basically one bedroom with an attached bathroom and closet and was definitely newer, given the LVP flooring and other modern fixtures. And he was looking forward to being in that bed with her later. "You shower first, I'll make some calls."

"Are you sure? You can go first." But she was already moving toward the bathroom.

"Oh, okay." He took a step in the direction of the bathroom.

She let out a short squeak and sprinted for it. "No way, I was lying." He laughed as she hovered in between the bed and bathroom. "Unless you really want the shower first?"

God, he wanted to kiss her again. "I was just messing with you. Go ahead. I'll see if I can get a hold of the search and rescue team."

"Ugh. We're going to have to fill out so much paperwork later," she said. Then she sobered slightly. "You think we're safe here?"

"I don't know. Without knowing who sent those drones... The parking lot was full so I think we're probably safer here than anywhere else. Whoever is doing this won't want witnesses." Too messy.

She nodded slowly. "Yeah, maybe."

"How about we shower and clean up—and eat—then regroup and

decide what to do?"

"Okay." Still looking pensive, she quietly shut the door behind her.

Instead of sitting on the bed, because he was so filthy, he picked up the landline to start making phone calls. Even though he could fantasize about joining Mari in the shower, he had to take care of this first. He had to make sure someone knew where they were and keep her safe.

CHAPTER 15

Bradford stepped into the kitchen of the tiny two bedroom, two bath cottage rental that they'd found on the outskirts of St. Francisville. It was right on a lake he was sure stayed busy in the summertime. Which, it was basically summer anyway, or close to it. "What smells so good?"

"Hope you like Greek and Lebanese food." Chance set down an oversized brown bag then started pulling out boxes.

"Hell yeah."

"Good, because I grabbed a little of everything."

Berlin was in the attached living room barely a few feet away watching the local news. "Better save me some baba ghanoush," she called out.

Chance didn't look up from unloading the different dishes. "I bought you extra, babe. And moussaka."

Berlin fist-pumped without turning away from the screen. "They've been talking about the search and rescue on the news. Only a little blip, but they mentioned it at least."

"Am I good to take the chicken shawarma?" Bradford asked, his gaze straying to the screen. The local news had shifted over to national news, so Berlin had muted it.

But he froze as a familiar face popped up on screen. "Hey, turn that up."

Food forgotten, he strode into the connected room and stood in front of the flat-screen as Berlin adjusted the volume.

The woman on screen had a somber expression as she continued talking... "A man has been charged with burning down ten new townhomes in Pigeon Forge, Tennessee. Recently built and still unoccupied, no lives were lost that police know of. But an investigation into the motive behind the arson is underway. They also believe that the man in custody was working with an accomplice, so any information..."

"What's the deal?" Berlin asked, pulling his attention away from the screen. "You know the firebug?"

"No." His attention was on the bottom of the screen, not the current story.

A small picture of an attractive woman was on the bottom right of the screen, teasing the next story. Hope Berkley.

His heart seized.

"Up next, the FBI is looking for answers into the potential disappearance of investigative journalist Hope Berkley. Berkley won a Pulitzer in 2022 for breaking open a bank fraud scandal..."

Disappearance? Bradford strode right out the front door, his cell in hand as he called Hope.

Her phone rang four times, then went to voicemail.

He called again. Same deal.

So he texted. Then he texted one of her backup burners that not many people knew about.

A minute later he received a text. *I'm okay. Don't worry about me.*

Yeah, that wasn't possible. Though the response was somewhat reassuring. *Where are you? I can help.*

He didn't receive a response, not that he'd expected one. But he'd had to offer regardless.

Reach out anytime. For anything. It was a standing offer, one he'd given her many times before. Then he added, *I'm stateside and have access to a private plane if you ever need one.*

He figured it was better to get specific with his offer. Because Hope was smart and determined, but when she was on a story, she was hyperfocused to the point where everything else fell away.

To his surprise, he got a response. *I might take you up on that.*

He blinked even as worry settled in his gut and took hold. Hope could take care of herself, no doubt about that. But she wasn't invincible, something he was pretty sure she forgot most of the time. Or she just had a death wish. He honestly didn't know, because she charged into things without seeming to be aware that she wasn't actually immortal.

Back inside, the news was still on but muted, and it had shifted to a story about the best beaches to visit this summer.

"So who was the woman on screen?" Berlin asked as he sat at the table with her and Chance.

It was clear that Chance nudged her under the table.

But Berlin wasn't going to let this go. He knew better than that. He was also surprised that she didn't already know who the woman was to him.

"You really don't know? I assumed you dug into all of us," he muttered as he started plating his food. Even though he didn't feel like eating, one of his mottos was *eat when you can because you never know when you'll get another meal.* That was more or less a military thing and very true.

"I looked into your military background, but I didn't dig into your personal stuff." And she sounded affronted that he didn't know that. "I only know what you've told me. And I thought we were friends," she added with a sniff. But he saw the hurt in her gaze.

And damn it, she was his friend. This was just the sort of thing he never talked about. “We are friends, B. And...Hope is my wife.”

Berlin’s bright blue-green eyes widened. “You mean...ex-wife?”

“Nope. Wife.”

Not that Hope seemed to give a damn about that. But she hadn’t served him with divorce papers yet so that was something.

CHAPTER 16

"I'm pretty sure anything would have been good at this point," Mari said as she leaned back in the chair, "but this shrimp and grits was amazing." Becky had brought them dinner straight to the cottage and told them to eat and rest. She was so glad they hadn't had to socialize with the other guests at the B&B in the cafeteria.

"No kidding." Colin yawned, even though it was only eight. He stood from the table and moved toward the window that faced the parking lot, pulled back the curtain.

He'd been doing that for the last hour, "just checking" he'd told her. He wanted to see if anyone new arrived and she figured it gave him something tangible to do.

The kitchen was small, just like the rest of the place. It was basically one big open room with the kitchen area flowing into the bedroom. There was also a closet and a bathroom, and yep, that was it.

The cottage was perfect for two people and she was trying not to obsess about the fact that there was one bed.

They were both adults so it was only a big deal if they made it one. And she refused to do that. At least they'd both showered and changed into their extra clothes. She'd left her dirty ones in the bathtub and was hoping the owners would let them wash their stuff tomorrow. She hadn't called anyone yet because her phone had been completely dead. So had Colin's.

"Someone's driving up," he murmured so she joined him at the window and pulled back the curtain just a bit to see too.

Using the landline, he'd called the local sheriff who'd promised to handle things with search and rescue. Eventually they'd have to do interviews, fill out paperwork, and she still needed to call Gary and let him know what was going on. She should have called him from the landline, but he must have heard by now what had happened. Once the rescue had started, since he was the owner of the plane, he'd have been contacted.

She knew Gary would be understanding. But she didn't want to deal with talking to anyone—especially someone whose two-million-dollar plane had been sabotaged. She didn't even want to think about how much it was going to cost to repair. He was going to have questions, and right now she didn't have the mental strength to answer any of them. Hell, she didn't even have answers other than someone planted an EMP.

Maybe it was selfish, but the guy was loaded. If he was really in a bind, he could rent a car or fly commercial.

"Nice Land Rover," she murmured, eyeing the vehicle as it parked a couple spots down from the front of their cottage.

Thanks to all the lighting surrounding the cottages, they could see the occupants clearly. A woman got out of the driver's seat and a man got out of the passenger. They were both wearing puffer vests, jeans and boots.

"He looks familiar," Mari murmured more to herself than Colin.

"Really?"

"Yeah."

The guy with dark hair pulled out two dark brown, likely leather weekender bags from the back before he slung his arm around the woman and kissed the top of her head.

"Maybe." Mari scrubbed her eyes and face and let the curtain fall back in place. "I'm so tired I don't know anything at this point."

"Becky said we could just leave our food outside the door."

"They're so nice," she said around a yawn. "You think the sheriff will stop by tonight?"

"I hope not." Colin picked up her now empty plate and stacked it on his. Then he set all their stuff on a tray outside the room and shut and locked the door.

She sighed in relief at the lock. "Do you have a preference for side of the bed?" she asked as she headed to the bathroom to brush her teeth. It gave her an excuse to avoid eye contact.

Because yeah, she was feeling weird after their kiss. Good weird. Weird weird. Maybe a little bad weird. Ugh, she didn't know how she felt.

She knew she'd liked the damn kiss, and that just annoyed her. She didn't do relationships, not really. She was so busy and loved her life the way it was. Loved flying. There were a couple guys she'd seen on and off over the years, but nothing had stuck. There was no permanence and she was okay with that. She refused to change her life to suit a man. Probably because she'd never met anyone who made her want more than some fun.

Until maybe...now she was thinking about more. More with Colin.

And yep, that annoyed her.

"Doesn't matter to me." He stepped into the bathroom with her and grabbed his own toothbrush. Now that he was cleaned up he smelled, well, as good as he had in the woods. What was that about? "Nice of her to provide all these toiletries." He lifted up the packaged toothbrush Becky had left for him.

Mari smiled around her own toothbrush. "I guess some of us are just more prepared," she said around a mouthful of toothpaste. She always packed a spare in her backpack. It was one of her true necessities.

He just snorted. "Says the woman who enjoyed sharing my tarp."

She spit out the toothpaste. "Fair enough." It was a little weird how not weird it was to be in the bathroom getting ready for bed with him.

And jeez, she needed to come up with a better word than weird.

Surreal, maybe? Because this was something couples did, something people in relationships did. And they weren't...anything. Barely friends again. She found her gaze straying to his mouth as he finished brushing his teeth and spit out his toothpaste, and desperately wanted a replay of that kiss. But she didn't want to stop.

"What are you thinking about?"

She blinked and realized he was watching her in the mirror with those soulful blue eyes. "About all the calls I need to make tomorrow," she lied. Then she paused when she heard a bunch of pings coming from the other room, breaking into their quiet haven. "I think my phone is working again, so maybe I'll have to make a few tonight."

Because real life was checking back in. She was thankful for the distraction, and the excuse to take the focus off being alone with Colin. Because if she gave in to what she wanted, she'd regret it once they got back to their real lives. And then things would be off between them yet again.

Another set of pings went off and he shook his head. "Same."

In the bedroom, she slid into the bed wearing her backup clothes because no way was she going to strip down and sleep in her underwear with him. So jeans and a T-shirt it was.

Colin eyed her as he slid into the other side of the bed. "Would it bother you if I took off my shirt? Seriously. I don't want to make you uncomfortable."

She lifted a shoulder as she pulled up the slew of text messages. "Go for it." Did she sound casual? She felt like she did, but she refused to look at him as he stripped his shirt off.

Okay, lies. She peeked out of the corner of her eye as he stripped and, of course, neatly folded it and set it with his now dry backpack.

Even his back was sexy and wasn't that annoying.

She quickly looked back at her phone out of self-preservation as he slid into bed next to her with a sigh.

She had a bunch of texts, including one from Gary—his had been annoyed at first, then worried once he'd clearly found out what happened. She tried calling him, but it wouldn't connect, and she was having a hell of a time focusing on anything besides Colin being half naked in the bed with her.

So she texted Gary, hoping it would go through. *I think you heard about your plane, looks like sabotage, not sure what's going on. Talking to the local police, trying to figure things out.* The last part wasn't technically true, but she would be talking to law enforcement soon enough.

He responded moments later. *It's fine, I'm just glad you're okay. Let me know if you need anything. And don't worry about the plane, I'll get it all sorted. There's a reason I've got insurance.*

She smiled, relief immediately sliding through her. She hadn't expected any different, but it was still nice that he cared.

Next she texted Berlin, who'd already texted her eight times. *We're okay, hunkering down at a B&B.*

Finally! Omg, we've been so worried. I couldn't even track your phone.

We've been in the middle of nowhere essentially. Service here sucks. But Colin talked to the sheriff so he knows we're okay. There was more to it, but Berlin didn't need all the little details.

I'm nearby with Chance and Bradford so let us know if you want us to pick you up. We rented a place and can head out tonight.

Mari paused, glanced over at Colin who'd shut his eyes after sending off a couple texts. He was breathing in and out in a steady rhythm. And fine, she loved the idea of curling up next to him. If they'd gone to that horse ranch, the obvious choice, then she might be worried that someone had tracked them down. But they'd gone way out of their way to come here instead and only the sheriff knew about their location. Still...maybe they should just head out tonight.

That might be a good idea. She quickly relayed what had happened with the drones, then waited for a response.

Only to realize that her message hadn't gone through and now there was a big X over where her bars were. Sighing, she set her phone back on the nightstand and closed her eyes.

She was just going to rest for a few minutes, then she'd try reaching out to Berlin again.

CHAPTER 17

Colin woke up to a warm, sexy woman plastered against his chest. It was about three in the morning according to the digital clock on the nightstand, but something had woken him and he wasn't sure what it was.

His damn brain, more than likely.

Actually, it was Mari's leg thrown over his middle as she wrapped her body around him. Her leg was tossed over his lower abdomen and oh, hell.

He shifted back slightly, making the bed squeak, and suddenly Mari's eyes opened. The room was dim, with only the illumination from the digital clock directed at the bed.

"Everything okay?" she murmured, glancing around the shadowy room.

His gaze fell to her mouth, and god, he hated himself a little. They were sleeping in this bed together only because of the situation. He needed to keep his shit together. Not be fantasizing about— He froze as he realized something. "There's no outside light," he whispered. "And no fan in the bathroom going." He'd left it on for white noise. Could be nothing, but he wasn't taking that chance.

Eyes now wide, she lifted a finger to her mouth then reached over and grabbed the digital clock. "Batteries," she whispered.

He eased out of bed and moved to the window where they'd eaten at the tiny table. And not for the first time he was cursing that he didn't have a weapon with him. As he flattened himself against the wall by the window, he saw Mari putting her shoes on.

At least they were on the same page—if something was going on, they needed to be ready to run at a moment's notice.

He didn't see anyone lurking in the shadows but all the lights that had been illuminating the cottages before were off.

In the distance, however, he could see lights by the horse barn. They didn't have a lot of options at this point for escape. And if someone wanted to strike at them now, they weren't just going to sit back and do nothing.

Moving quickly, he put on his own shoes, shirt, then grabbed his backpack, leaving his dirty clothes behind.

He motioned to Mari to move with him and they both ducked into the bathroom.

"Should we call the police?" she asked.

"We can but it'll take them forever to get out here." This place was so far removed from town. And right now, he hadn't even seen a threat.

Her eyes lit up. "Berlin is close by," she whispered suddenly, as if just remembering. "She's with two of the Redemption Harbor Security guys." She had her phone out as she spoke but he knew before she said anything that she had no service by her disappointed expression.

He held out his own phone for her to see, the little screen the only illumination in the room now. No service. They might as well be on the moon.

"We're out of options," he whispered. "We can sit tight—"

"Hell no."

Yeah, he hadn't been planning on that either. "Or we climb out the back window and head out on foot."

She nodded.

"There's a risk that someone will take us out so I'm going first. If something happens to me, shoot anyone you see with the flare gun. It might give you enough time to get away."

It was clear that she didn't like the sound of that, but she nodded. Then she ducked out of the bathroom before he could stop her and was back moments later, a wine bottle opener in hand. The old-school kind.

He lifted an eyebrow.

She shrugged and clutched it tightly in her hand. "Work with what you've got."

Fair enough.

He grabbed a hand mirror from one of the drawers, then they both stepped into the shower together. He eased open the window inside it, grateful when it didn't make much noise. After opening it, he waited a beat. Then, heart racing, he held out the mirror slowly to check in both directions.

He didn't see anyone, though that didn't mean a sniper wasn't waiting for them. And yeah, maybe he was letting his mind run away with him, but he'd been under fire before and something was off. He felt it to his bones. There was no storm currently and only the cottages seemed to have lost power.

Walking into the unknown was a nightmare when you knew what could be waiting.

He slid off his pack and handed it to Mari. Then he motioned that he was climbing through and for her to pass it to him.

As he shimmied through the small opening, he swore he could feel a bull's-eye on him, but as he landed on his feet he quickly took in his surroundings. Their cottage was at the end of the row, with the window facing the woods.

"Hold on," he whispered as he took his backpack and set it down.

He moved to the edge of the building and held the mirror out again. The antebellum mansion was behind the cottage but from this angle he could see the rest of the cottages in the mirror.

No movement, but it was damn dark out so that didn't mean anything.

By the time he turned back around, Mari was slipping through the window, butt first.

He moved fast, holding on to her hips as he helped her settle on her feet.

No one, he mouthed, pointing in the direction of the mansion.

She nodded and pointed toward the parking area around the front of their cabin. The horse barn was past the parking lot and he had a feeling their best escape option was that way.

He stepped in front of her, mirror out and barely slid it around the corner—and froze at what he spotted.

The two people they'd seen arrive in the Land Rover were at the cottage's front door, weapons in hand. Both had silencers. One man, one woman. The guy was bending down, likely picking the lock.

Colin plastered himself to the back of the wall and held up a finger to his mouth.

Eyes wide, Mari nodded.

He was going to wait until they were inside, then they'd have to make a break for it and hope they weren't seen. At least it was dark outside, with the half-moon and stars—which were a lot brighter out in the country—their main source of illumination.

He waited a beat. Two. Three. Then he held the mirror out again and saw the armed individuals slipping inside.

He leaned in close to Mari and whispered, "Two people from the Land Rover have weapons. We need to run for the barn, try to find a way to escape now."

Jaw tight, she nodded.

He stepped out from behind cover first, his heart racing. They'd shut the door behind them.

"Now."

They sprinted full speed across the small parking lot toward the connecting path. He felt like they were as loud as elephants but there was no way around it.

They needed to put distance between them and those assassins, or whoever they were, and fast.

Sprinting flat out, they moved farther around the path toward the horse barn. Once they reached a fence line with a natural hedge of what looked like miniature Christmas trees, he ducked down, pulling Mari with him.

She was still clutching her wine bottle opener with the jagged corkscrew held out like a blade.

"Did you see anyone else?" he asked.

Breathing uneven, she shook her head.

He peered between two of the mini trees and spotted the couple by the back of their vehicle. Colin and Mari were too far away to hear, but the man pointed toward the woods and the woman took off. Then the man headed in the direction of the curving path, no doubt heading for the barn. Because where else would they go?

"In here," he murmured, and they both ducked behind the hedges. "If I get a chance, I'm taking him out." Because his hands were as much a weapon as anything else.

Mari looked like she wanted to argue, but nodded and ducked down.

He slid off his backpack and crouched low. The prickly foliage was the perfect cover, even if it jabbed through their clothes.

Colin heard the man approaching, his steps making quiet footfalls on the worn dirt path. The man moved past them.

"Should we follow?" Mari whispered once they couldn't hear him anymore.

Colin shook his head. Though he'd love to take out the threat, he preferred they didn't have any contact with either of the unknown targets. They could be working with others for all they knew.

And this way these assailants wouldn't know when they'd left. Hopefully it would give him and Mari an advantage.

About five minutes later the man returned down the path, talking quietly. Maybe into an earpiece.

"They're not at the barn, and the horses were undisturbed." Then he paused and said, "They couldn't have gone far on foot."

Colin and Mari waited another sixty seconds, then cautiously exited the hedges. Once they saw it was clear, they raced toward the barn. Inside, there were a handful of horses, including Biscuit.

One of them snuffled slightly at their presence, but seemed otherwise unbothered by them. As Colin debated if they should take two of the horses and escape, Mari nodded at the final stall with an oversized door. No horse inside, but there was a side-by-side and a small ATV.

And bless these people, the keys were hanging on the hook by the door. He snagged both of them, then disabled the side-by-side as Mari, clearly understanding, slid onto the front of the ATV. It was smaller which meant they could go places the side-by-side wouldn't allow.

As soon as he slid on behind her, she started the engine.

They'd just given away their location, but there was no way around it. And no time to lose.

Wind rushed over them as Mari revved the engine and they shot out of the open back door of the barn. He glanced over his shoulder as they raced along the wide pathway toward the tree line.

Right as they disappeared into the woods, he spotted the two gun-toting assholes racing toward the barn.

CHAPTER 18

"That way." Colin pointed to the side as the ATV sputtered again.

They'd made it roughly forty miles from the barn, which was decent considering they'd been riding over rough terrain. But the ATV was about out of gas and they needed to hide it before they headed out on foot.

They'd left some tracks, but after they'd gone off-road, there was no way the two people could have followed them in the Land Rover. The paths were too narrow and there were too many trees for big vehicles to maneuver through.

Mari headed for the cluster of rocks and trees just before the ATV sputtered one last time and died. She let out a growl of frustration, but they both got off and stretched even as they took in their surroundings.

"I know where we are," he murmured as he rolled the ATV under a small rock overhang. "Or I'm relatively sure I know where we are."

"This doesn't even feel like Louisiana." Mari looked up at the twenty-five-foot rock face in front of them. "Is that a waterfall I hear in the distance?"

"Yeah. There are about forty or so around here. We're in the Clark Creek or Tunica Falls area. It straddles the Louisiana and Mississippi state line.

In the thick of spring and summer there are a lot of hikers out here, so we'll probably see some in a couple hours."

"I was hoping we'd be out of here in a couple hours." Mari's tone was dry as she looked back at him, the moonlight perfectly illuminating her.

"If we're lucky but...I don't know. We might have to hunker down somewhere if they managed to follow us." He grabbed a huge fallen branch with dead leaves covering it and moved it in front of the ATV.

Mari saw what he was doing and did the same, picking up fallen branches and other foliage that they built up around it in what he hoped was a natural way.

"Better than nothing," he muttered as they looked at their handiwork.

"So which way?" Mari snapped her backpack in place, looking ready to take on anything.

Even after this shitstorm, she was incredible under pressure. He'd been attracted to her for a long time, and he'd always liked her. That like was turning into something a lot stronger the more time he spent with her. This was the kind of woman a sane man didn't walk away from, the kind of person who had your back no matter what. "You would have been great in the military."

She blinked at the random statement. "What?"

"I was just thinking about how great you are under pressure," he said as he motioned east.

"Oh. Thank you. I'd have been pretty terrible though. I don't think I would have taken orders very well."

He snorted softly at that. "Probably not."

"So why this way?" she asked as they trekked down a lightly worn trail. It wasn't that wide, but there was evidence of some foot traffic.

"We're going to head toward the waterfall. There should be trail markers near most of the falls. From there, we'll follow the trail until we get to the trailhead."

"Any park rangers or…whatever, at these places?"

"Unfortunately no. Too many bullshit budget cuts," he muttered. And this place had always been understaffed on a good day. "Last time I was here, the few places I hiked at had small parking lots and a box to place your payment for parking in." All very rudimentary.

As they started toward the first waterfall, clouds drifted in front of the moon, blocking a portion of their light so they pulled out their small flashlights to light the way.

They were both quiet as they walked, both alert for any danger, though he was pretty certain they'd lost their pursuers back at the B&B. For now, anyway.

But as they hiked up a steep hillside, Mari clicked off her flashlight.

Without asking questions, he did too. Had she heard or seen something?

She turned to him and held up her finger to her mouth, then pointed in front of her before she crouched down.

He moved with her, crawling to the edge of the hillside where there was a drop of about twenty feet.

And that was when he heard the low murmur of voices.

Adrenaline surged through him as they inched to the edge. He peered over, grateful for the cloud cover and shadows of the forest.

A man was visible by the edge of a pool of water, his back to them. "We're looking. No sign of either of them. But they have to show up sometime. We drew a perimeter and there's only so far they could have gotten. Adina is on the other trail, and if she can't find them, she'll just wait at the trailhead." He paused again. Then, "I know how important this is. Yes," the man gritted out. "I'll get what we need from the woman. If we can't find her, we'll bring out the drones at daybreak."

Next to him, Mari tensed, but was otherwise silent.

What the hell was going on? *Get what they need from the woman?* This sounded like more than coming after her for an overheard conversation. Not that he'd ever thought that was the reason for whatever this bullshit was. To be fair, he had no idea what this was about but now they knew it was definitely about Mari. They wanted something from her. But what?

"We're both professionals. Yes. Yes, I *know*," he gritted out again. Then he hung up and cursed as he stalked toward another trail. As he did, he called someone else. Maybe this Adina. "Anything?" Pause. "Same." Then he hung up and continued heading west toward what looked like another waterfall.

"Want to follow him and kill him?" Mari whispered.

Blinking, he stared at her.

"Or rough him up, whatever." She rolled her eyes, but he could see the fear flickering in them.

"While I would love to bash that guy's face in"—especially for threatening Mari—"we need to get distance from him."

As they stood, Mari accidentally kicked a few rocks over the edge.

They both froze at the noise.

Quickly, he tugged her behind a large oak and then he ducked behind two pine trees. Using the gap between them, he peered in the direction the man had gone.

Moments later, a large shadow moved along the tree line. Colin couldn't make out the man, but it had to be him. The guy was quiet, he'd give him that.

Eventually the shadow disappeared. Or maybe the guy was waiting them out. Either way, they couldn't stay here forever like sitting ducks now that they'd given themselves away.

He motioned to Mari to step back from the tree and they'd head back the way they'd come. It meant they'd have to go around a longer trail to get out of the woods, but after hearing the guy on the phone, they needed to avoid the trailhead anyway.

A shot broke through the quiet night air, slamming into a tree ten feet away. Wood splintered under the impact as he shoved Mari to the ground, covering her body with his.

Pop. Pop. Pop.

More gunfire erupted as they crawled far enough down the hillside so that they were out of sight from their shooter.

"It'll take him a while to climb or go around," Colin rasped out as they sprinted through the woods. "For now let's stay off the direct path until we absolutely have to. I saw a place we can hide out for a while."

Jaw tight, Mari nodded and jumped over a fallen tree. "I bet killing that guy doesn't sound so bad now."

It was probably wrong that he loved how bloodthirsty she was, but yeah, he was having second thoughts. Because no one was hurting Mari on his watch.

CHAPTER 19

"This doesn't look good," Bradford murmured from the back seat of the SUV as they arrived at the bed-and-breakfast. A sheriff's car was in the parking lot, the lights flashing, but no siren on.

They'd contemplated coming earlier, but Berlin had hacked into the local sheriff's department and confirmed that Colin had contacted the guy, and that he and Mari were staying at a nearby place. Everything had seemed good, but now he was wondering if they should have done things differently.

"Everyone follow my lead," Berlin said as she parked next to the sheriff's car.

At least there weren't ambulances or fire trucks or anything else. Just the sheriff—he recognized him from his picture online—and the two owners of the bed-and-breakfast who he also recognized from pictures Berlin had found online.

Berlin was out of the vehicle before either he or Chance had unstrapped.

"You're a brave man, getting engaged to her," Bradford murmured.

"I think you mean lucky."

He snickered as they got out of the vehicle. "Whatever word you want to use, you're braver than me." Because Berlin was terrifying.

Not that there'd ever been any attraction between them. No, his heart had been taken a long time ago and he never wanted it back. Hell, at this point he'd learned to live without it.

"If y'all are here to check in—"

Berlin gently cut off Rebecca Canfield, one of the owners. "We're here to find our friends. Their plane went down yesterday and they managed to make it here. I spoke to Mari last night but haven't heard from her or Colin since then." Berlin's voice was full of concern—and Bradford knew she wasn't acting.

They were all worried.

"I'm Becky," she said to Berlin. "And yes, your friends were here last night—"

"Your friends stole an ATV and disabled another from what we can tell," the sheriff interrupted, earning an annoyed glance from Becky. "And they cut the power in the middle of the night, causing all sorts of havoc. The owners are also now having to deal with lost food because of the fridges and freezers that went out."

"Our generators kicked in," Becky murmured. "It's fine."

"If they took an ATV, it was because they were in danger," Bradford said as he stepped up next to Berlin. He held his hand out to the sheriff, who took it cautiously. "I'm Bradford. We work with Mari. She's one of our contract pilots and it's our understanding that someone sabotaged her plane. We have reason to believe she and Colin are in danger. So I promise you, if they took something, it was because they had no other choice."

"They looked rough when they arrived," Becky's husband, John, said.

"Have any of your other guests checked out? Or did anyone see anything?"

"Now see here—"

"Hush, Robert," Becky said to the sheriff. "You already told us that the FAA is investigating something, so it sounds like someone did mess with their plane." Becky rolled her eyes, then added, "He's my baby brother, I can talk to him like that."

"Becky—"

"No. It felt wrong that those two just up and left in the middle of the night. I trust my gut with people, and I liked them. And what a cute couple. It made no sense that they split like that in the middle of the night." She looked at the three of them. "They took their backpacks but left their dirty clothes behind and it seems like they might have climbed out the bathroom window. There were two shoe prints on the windowsill." She shrugged as the sheriff made a surprised sound. "I didn't get around to telling you yet."

"Look, we run an investigative firm in New Orleans, and we've assisted the police there many times," Bradford said even though Berlin had told him to let her take the lead. "You can call Detective Camila Flores to confirm. We're worried about our friends, that's all. And if it's about the ATV, we'll pay for it."

"That thing is over twenty years old, it's fine," Becky said before her husband could respond—and he clearly wanted to. "We're not pressing charges. If anything, now I'm actually worried about them."

"Did anyone check in after them?" Berlin asked.

"And are they still here?" Chance added.

The sheriff looked at his sister, apparently wanting an answer to that too.

"Well, one couple checked in about an hour after they got here, but they're already gone. It didn't even look like they slept in their beds."

"Did they make an online reservation?" Berlin asked.

The sheriff shot her an annoyed look but then raised an eyebrow at his sister.

"No, they called and said they were driving through and were hoping to crash for a couple hours. We had one extra room and they said they were only staying one night."

"I'll need their info," the sheriff said to his sister, then looked at the three of them. "And no more questions from any of you. I'll be reaching out to this Detective Flores, but this isn't your investigation."

"Our friends are missing," Bradford growled. "We're not just leaving."

"Fine. Are you staying somewhere local?"

Bradford nodded.

"Good. Give me your information and I'll reach out if I need anything."

That was a brush-off if he'd ever heard one, but it wasn't as if they could stand around and argue with the guy. Now they had information at least.

"What kind of gas mileage does your ATV get?" Chance asked. "And do you know what direction they went in?"

The sheriff shook his head. "Damn it—"

"It had about an hour's worth of gas left in it if that's what you're asking, and from the tracks, it looks like they headed east. Our property butts up against the national forest in that direction." Becky helpfully pointed for them.

The sheriff ran a hand over his face, clearly exhausted with his sister. "Okay, that's it. No more questions. It's time for you three to leave."

At least they had something to go on. And as the three of them got back into the SUV, Bradford heard Becky say, "You're just grumpy because you haven't had any coffee yet."

CHAPTER 20

"This way," Mari whispered, pointing at the waterfall. They'd been running for the last hour and now that the sun was cresting the eastern horizon, she heard a drone somewhere overhead. She just couldn't tell what direction it was coming from. And she still had no idea why two armed people were after her and Colin. "If we wade through there, we won't leave any tracks."

Colin nodded, then to her surprise, scooped her up before he stepped into the knee-high waters, his long legs making a lot faster strides than hers ever could have over the jutting rocks. Her stomach flipped as he held her close, his big arms wrapping around her tight. She wanted to burrow into him, close her eyes and block out this nightmare.

He was moving fast, his body vibrating with tension as they hurried toward the pounding waterfall. It wasn't huge, but it completely spanned the front of the twenty-foot-wide rock face and—

She held her breath as he rushed through the pounding water, the shock of the cold stunning her.

The rush of the water was louder on the back side of the falls, but not terrible.

"Stay here," he said, though it was hard to hear over the pounding falls, and set her on the jutting base of rock that ran the entire length under the falls.

When she nodded he dumped his backpack on the smooth rock next to her, then disappeared back behind the curtain of water.

Now her own tension ratcheted up as she waited, counting the seconds until his return. One, two, three... She got to forty-five seconds by the time he reappeared.

Relief punched through her immediately at the sight of him, his T-shirt molded to his chest and abs. He ran his hands through his hair to get some of the wetness out, then stripped off his shirt, setting it on the rock next to her.

"Did you see anything?" she asked, trying not to stare. Now was definitely not the time to be checking him out, but come on. She had eyes. And he was gorgeous. She deserved a medal for sleeping next to him last night without doing anything.

He shook his head. "No, but I could hear a drone in the distance. I couldn't tell which direction, but I think this is a good place to hang tight for a while. We can't outrun drones in this terrain. The trees are getting too thin."

"Should we wait until dark again?" She hated the idea of just staying in place like sitting ducks, but could also see the appeal of hiding out here.

"I think we might have to. I couldn't see you at all when I was out there, at least from my angle. That's what took me so long, I wanted to see if the two hunting us would spot us. And since we walked over rocks to get here, there are no tracks. This is a solid place to hide out."

More mentally exhausted than physically, she nodded. "I don't hate this idea."

"How much food do you have?" he asked as he unzipped his own wet backpack.

Shivering against the cold and wet of her clothes sticking to her body, she unzipped her own and pulled out her plastic bag of protein bars. She'd also tucked her cell phone and a few other things into the gallon Ziploc bag. "Four protein bars. Not bad." She was running low on water but had two bottles. As she pulled out one of the bars, her cell phone slid out onto the rock.

"Shit." She went to grab her phone as it plunged down into the pool of water below. "Balls," she muttered.

Colin plucked it out of the water and set it far behind her even as she started scooting away from the edge, dragging her stuff with her. The ledge was about ten feet back, more than enough space for them to spread out.

"Can't believe I did that," she muttered.

"It's fine. I've still got my cell." He looked at his own, frowned. "Not that it matters, because there's still no signal. Here." He handed her the bar she'd dropped on the rock, then took one for himself. "Let's eat, then stretch out and try to get dry and warm. And I swear this isn't a line, but if you want to get out of your wet clothes and curl up with me, it wouldn't hurt to share our body warmth."

She snort-laughed even as her teeth chattered. "Hopefully mine'll still work when it dries out." It was touted as being water resistant but time would tell. Without the warmth of the sun in this cold, damp cave, there was no way she was getting warm without him. Or even dry. "Fine," she managed to get out, the cold overwhelming.

Even though she felt vulnerable, she stripped down to her bra and panties and was immediately glad not to have her wet clothes sticking to her. And if she was being really honest with herself, she was glad she had on matching undergarments, even as she inwardly berated herself.

So not important!

Colin took over, wringing out her clothes and setting them next to his in a corner that looked the dryest. And he wasn't a perv either. No sneaky looks, something she appreciated. Apparently she needed to be more like him, because she was struggling not to stare at his chest. And arms.

And lower.

Nope. Closing her eyes, she laid her head on her wet backpack and sighed. "This sucks."

She felt his big body moving in behind her, then he wrapped her up in all that strength and warmth, and god, she couldn't remember ever feeling this safe and protected. She was so used to taking care of herself—hyper-independent as her friends liked to say—but having a partner in all this was unexpectedly wonderful.

"I'm glad you're here with me," she whispered, wondering if he could even hear her.

He shifted slightly behind her and dragged his backpack under his head. "I'm glad I'm with you too. If you think you can get some sleep, go for it. I'll stay awake."

She nodded as a wave of exhaustion swept through her with a vengeance. They'd woken up in the middle of the night only to go on the run from gun-wielding assholes. Then they'd had to run again when they'd been spotted. And even though she hated to admit it, she was tired. Just bone-deep exhausted and scared out of her mind that those strangers would find them, and shoot them.

Would anyone even discover their bodies? Would their would-be killers give their families closure, or would they dump them somewhere no one would ever locate? She shuddered at the thought and Colin's grip around her tightened.

"It's going to be okay," he murmured right next to her ear.

A shiver rolled through her, and going on instinct, she turned in his arms, ignoring how uncomfortable she was against the rock.

He sucked in a breath as she wrapped her arm around him, going skin to skin, her skimpy bra not much of a barrier.

"Is this okay?"

He let out a strangled sound, but that was a definite nod.

And okay, she liked his reaction. If anything, it took her mind off the outside world and the shitstorm that was awaiting them if they left too soon.

But that wasn't what this was about and she knew it. She was attracted to Colin in a way she'd never experienced before, and had been for far longer than she wanted to admit. She just plain liked him as a person. And as she wrapped around him, warmth spread throughout her entire body, her nipples pulling into tight points against her bra cups at the intimate contact.

Slowly, she slid her hand up and down his back, savoring the feel of all his strength underneath her fingertips, wondering what she was doing and how far he'd let her go. And if he would touch her, relieve the ache pulsing between her legs.

When his big hand settled on her hip and tightened, heat flared in his gaze as he looked at her. "What are you doing?"

"I don't know," she whispered, but he must have heard her above the falls.

"Your timing sucks."

She shrugged even as a grin tugged at her lips. He wasn't wrong. But actual death might be at their doorstep and they had nowhere to go right now. She didn't want to die without tasting Colin Lockhart. She had been fighting her attraction to him forever, denying herself what she really wanted, and was tired of the battle.

As if he read her mind, he groaned and crushed his mouth to hers.

He tasted like the chocolate protein bar and now she was forever going to associate chocolate with his kisses.

She tried to be quiet, but didn't think it mattered considering the deluge of water pounding down around them. They couldn't hear anything outside this little cavern so no one else could hear them.

She nipped his bottom lip, grinned as he rolled his hips against her—and felt his very real reaction. Oh god, that gave her a rush, knowing that he was reacting to her. And who knew how much time they had, if they'd even make it out of here.

He wasn't looking at her like she was his best friend's kid sister. Nope, he was holding on to her and kissing her like he'd been dying to. The exact way she'd fantasized about for ages.

And when he slid his hand up to cup her breast, started teasing her nipple through the wet fabric, she might have let out a moan. A long, needy one.

She was grateful for the waterfall, hoped it covered how desperate she must sound. Because she was absolutely desperate for more of him. The man got under her skin in a way no one else ever had. And it wasn't like she was going to analyze that, but good god, she wanted to take some pleasure from him if this was their last day on earth.

As he rolled her hard nipple, she palmed the front of his boxer briefs, enjoyed the way he jerked against her, pushing into her touch. Oh yeah, he wanted this as much as she did, and she could already feel heat building deep inside her, a release on the horizon if she could just stop thinking and let go.

Maybe, later, once they were hopefully out of this mess, she'd second-guess herself, but right now they deserved to find pleasure in each other.

Thankfully he didn't pull back, didn't try to slow things down. Instead, he slid his hand lower, lower, until he delved between her thighs and began teasing between her already slick folds.

She jerked against him as he found her clit, began rubbing in tight little circles. That desperation from before was next-level now, her need building as he continued teasing her. She threw one leg over his outer thigh to give him better access as she dipped her hand down the front of his boxer briefs.

When she squeezed his hard length, he reacted with his whole body. Oh yeah, he loved that. So she did it again, then began stroking him in hard, even strokes as he did the same between her legs.

It didn't take long until she was coming against his long, talented fingers in the quickest, rawest orgasm she'd ever had. She shouldn't have been able to come like this on a rock-hard surface while they were running for their lives.

But this was Colin, the man who'd starred in her earliest fantasies.

Tearing his mouth from hers, he buried his face against her neck and groaned as he came against her hand in jerky, wild thrusts.

She wasn't sure how long they lay there like that, but eventually they pulled back and she wondered if things would be awkward. But instead, he kissed her long and sweet before he tugged her to him.

"Let's clean up, then rest," he murmured against the top of her head.

And she was more than okay with that. She had a feeling she'd be able to actually rest with him holding her.

CHAPTER 21

Colin could feel the tension inside him kicking up as it got darker and darker beyond the waterfall. They'd been inside the cave all day, sleeping for most of it so they were at least rested. But they had no water and no food left. If they got desperate, he could capture some water and filter it through sand and charcoal, but he hoped it didn't come to that.

And Mari's phone was useless. He had a little juice in his, but there wasn't much left so they had to conserve it.

"I hate waiting like this." Sitting with her legs crossed and her backpack already on, Mari was as ready as he was to get out of here.

But he wanted to leave at twilight. There wouldn't be any drones out then—or there shouldn't be. Though there was a chance their pursuers would have night vision drones, something he couldn't do anything about.

Once they left the cave, they'd still have some light to get out of the waterfall and pool area. From there, he had a good idea of exactly how to get to the road that led in and out of the national park. "I know." He slid his own backpack on, but it was still too soon to leave. Might as well make conversation to pass the time, and there was one thing that had been on his mind. "So you held on to a grudge for pretty long with me."

She shot him a surprised look. "You deserved it."

They hadn't talked about earlier when they'd both brought each other to climax, and since she wasn't bringing it up, he'd opted not to either. But things weren't over between them, not by a long shot. Now that he'd had a taste of her, he just wanted more. Like, say, *forever*. "I know. And I wasn't chastising you or whatever. I'm impressed. So...is this like a thing with you?"

"A thing?" She cocked an eyebrow at him.

And god, he really did love everything about the feisty woman. "Yeah, holding grudges. Evan said something about it, and I remember you being pissed at one of your cousins for years. Jessica, I think?"

"She stole my Charizard card. Of course I was mad. Then she traded it for a really crappy one which made her thievery even worse."

"Weren't you in fourth grade?"

"Yep. But we're good now. Though I did steal an entire lunchbox of her Pokémon cards as payment."

He blinked.

She shrugged. "I considered it karma. I traded those cards to get my Charizard back—which I still have to this day."

He snorted lightly. "So I know never to mess with you."

"That's right, or you'll face Kim justice."

"Kim justice?"

"How has my brother never told you about Kim justice?" she asked, rocking back slightly as she laughed with her whole body.

He loved seeing her like this, and knew for this stolen moment she wasn't thinking about being hunted, but was just in this moment with him.

The waterfall was even louder now, so it was hard to hear and he found himself watching her lips move. Just reading her lips, he told himself. Not imagining kissing them. Or watching them close around his—

"If someone messes with one of us, they get Kim justice. My mom started it when some racist bitch tried to keep my brothers out of a play group."

"Your sweet mom?"

She blinked, then snort-laughed. "My mom is a freaking tiger. If you mess with her kids, she'll claw your face off. She got this woman's husband blackballed from a couple events until she got an apology. She still never liked the woman, and eventually the woman's oldest got kicked out of school for bad behavior and they ended up moving. Anyway, that's how 'Kim justice' started. Evan's the one who gave it a nickname and it sort of snowballed from there..." She shrugged, grinning in a way she never did when she talked about her mom.

"How are you and your mom doing?"

She let out a sigh. "Okay, I guess. She still gives me grief about not being married, but it's not as bad as it used to be. She's finally retiring—ish, and ready for her 'Halmi era' as she likes to call it. Being a grandmother has really mellowed her out in a way I *never* could have imagined just a decade ago."

"I get grief for not being married too," he said dryly. "From your mom as well as mine," he added.

Which made her snicker. "Yeah, I've heard them talk about you. 'Why can't he find a nice girl and settle down? Maybe it's a pilot thing? Look at Mari. She's still single too. Tsk, tsk.'" She shook her head. "I swear she just wants to blame anything and everything on me being a pilot." Her tone was light, but he hated the underlying pain in her voice.

Why did families have to be so complicated? So he changed the subject. "What other forms of vengeance have you enacted over the years?"

"Well...I did tell the girls' JV lacrosse team that I overheard you telling Evan about some issues you had..." She pointed between her legs. "I might have used the words 'super gonorrhea.' I figured they'd pass it on to the varsity team."

His mouth fell open.

"Hey, it's only after you told that jerk that I had an STI. Fair's fair. Kim justice, baby."

He grinned. "That actually explains a few weird conversations I've had over the years. Damn, Mari, you are brutal."

"My junior year, this girl Lynda—'Lynda with a y'," she said, rolling her eyes. "She put dark red paint on my chair to make it look like I'd started my period. I had no idea until Magnolia saw it and told me. Later I found out it had been intentional and all because some guy she liked, liked me instead. Freaking high school," she said, shaking her head.

"What did you do to her?"

"I let the air out of one of her tires. I kept doing it until she ended up getting a new tire. I actually felt bad about that one."

"You're smiling."

"Okay, as an adult I now kinda sorta feel bad about that one. It was driving her so crazy that she ended up putting an air pump in her trunk."

"So the lesson is to never mess with Mari." Or apparently her entire family.

"Yep." She looked out at the waterfall, her expression pensive. "Are we ready yet?"

"Yeah. I'm going to go first. I'll duck down and swim out, assess the situation. If it looks clear, I'll come back for you." He slid his backpack off even though he'd just put it back on. It wouldn't make sense to bring it for this visual recon.

"I don't like you doing all the scouting."

"Too bad." He slid into the small pool of water, which was chillier than it had been only an hour ago, glad he'd at least remembered to leave his shoes off. Getting out of here really was going to suck.

After ducking down, he swam under the water, going deeper as he made his way toward where he knew a shelf of rocks overhung the pool. Slowly, he surfaced, his eyes not taking long to adjust to the twilight as he scanned the water around him, the small shore area and the trees beyond.

At least the forest wasn't thick here, though it was getting dark. He eased a little more out of the water, listening and watching.

No buzzing overhead, though to be fair he mostly heard the pounding waterfall. But he couldn't see any movements along the shoreline or in the trees.

It was time to go. They had to risk it.

By the time he got Mari and his backpack, and they'd quietly made their way to the trees—as quietly as possible while dripping wet—the sun had completely set. They were both now dripping wet, cold, and the temperature would drop through the night. They had to get moving.

"We stick together," he whispered. "And if I say run, you run. One of us needs to make it out of here." He would rather it be her, but he kept that to himself. But there was no way he was letting her get hurt on his watch. Or ever.

She hesitated, but nodded. And he just hoped that if the time came, she actually would run and not stay and fight.

***

"Now what are y'all doing out here after dark?" the older man with a dusty Chevy asked as he eyed Mari and Colin on the side of the two-lane highway. "It's not safe to be on the side of the road once the sun goes down."

Ever since finally making it to the main road, they'd been walking for the last hour and she'd been about to give up hope that anyone would ever drive by. It was so damn dark out here at night. She didn't even want to think about what it would have been like to be alone. At least their clothes were mostly dry, but her feet ached and she wanted a shower. And food. And to punch Ackerman in the throat.

"We were hiking and got lost," Mari said in her sweetest voice as she took Colin's hand in hers. She was just acting, she told herself, but she liked his strength and warmth. She'd never been the kind of person to hold hands with a significant other but she loved holding on to his, feeling as if they were a real unit. "We were trying to see the falls and got turned around. And then I'm pretty sure I saw a bear and we just got lost."

The man looked unimpressed, but at least he'd pulled over for them. "Well, it's not far to town, but you're gonna get hit by a car if you keep walking along this road. It's too dark out here."

"Would you mind giving us a ride?" she asked.

Colin was a strong, silent sentinel behind her.

"Yeah, but you're both riding in the bed." He jerked a thumb at the back of this truck. Two bales of hay were in it and she didn't even care.

He had two golden retrievers in his truck, so she figured he probably wasn't a serial killer. She waved at the dogs. "You're the most beautiful babies I've ever seen."

She saw the man's face thaw just a little before they jumped into the back.

The two dogs stuck their head through the open window, so she got to pet them as she leaned up against Colin. He had his arms tight around her, holding her close, and she couldn't decide if she loved or hated how damn solid and wonderful he was.

For so many years she'd hung on to anger, and yeah, she knew it was healthy to let it go. But now he was in this new category and she wasn't sure how to handle it. He was in her head, and if she was stupid, he'd end up in her heart.

And that way lay madness.

She didn't have time for a relationship—not that he was offering one—and especially with her brother's best friend. Seriously, it would screw up the dynamics. She wasn't interested in changing herself or her lifestyle to suit a man. Not after everything she'd done to build her life. But...she really, really liked being with him. Even during all this madness, she was so damn glad to be with him.

"What are their names?" she called through the open window as the man pulled up to a four way stop.

"Sunshine and Marshmallow... My wife named them."

He sounded almost embarrassed, so she smothered the laugh that wanted to bubble up. "I bet I know who is who," she said to the dogs, including the one who she swore was smiling at her. She had to be Sunshine. She buried her hands in their fur and fought the sudden urge to cry.

All day she and Colin had been in this state of tense waiting.

Waiting to be discovered.

To be killed.

And she was still scared, but almost in an abstract way. She didn't know for sure who was after them, or why.

"You can drop us at the motel," Colin said through the window, his grip around her tightening slightly.

The dogs tucked their heads back into the truck as their owner made a turn toward The Red Apple motel. Though with a few lights out, so it said *ed ppl*. At least the apple itself was lit up, but this was the kind of place that rented by the hour, she was sure.

After the man—who'd never given them his name, she realized—dropped them off, she fell in step with Colin. "Is your phone working?"

He nodded as he looked down at it.

"Okay, good. I'll call Berlin, see if she's nearby." They weren't in St. Francisville, but a neighboring town. And from the looks of it, this place was a little rougher around the edges.

He nodded, glancing around the parking lot. "I'll grab us a room so we're not standing out here for everyone to see."

As he went inside, she ducked into the shadows of an out of order vending machine and called Berlin.

"Hello?"

Relief hit her. "It's me, Mari. I'm on Colin's phone."

"Are you guys okay? Where are you?"

"Ah, at The Red Apple Motel. Just got dropped off by some farmer. And yes, we're okay, for now. But there are definitely people after us," she whispered as a big rig truck rumbled past on the road, the noise cutting through the relative quiet.

Colin stepped out then, an old-fashioned key in hand. He nodded at her as she talked to Berlin, so she fell in step with him.

"We're only half an hour from you guys," Berlin said, and Mari could hear movement in the background. "Our SUV is already loaded up so we're heading out now. Do you have a room?"

She nodded as they stopped in front of the last one. "109, right on the end." She desperately wanted a hot shower and dry clothes.

"Sit tight, we're coming to get you."

"Should we call the cops?"

"Hell no. I don't know if they're being monitored or not. We'll see you soon."

"Okay. Bye." For the first time all day, Mari could see a light at the end of the tunnel. She also wondered where they went from here...and what happened between her and Colin once they got back to their real lives.

CHAPTER 22

"I desperately want a shower." Mari glanced at the bathroom door in the motel room.

The place wasn't god awful, but it wasn't great either. She wasn't even going to sit down on the bed, or in the little dining area. The bathroom was the only thing sparkling in here.

"Go ahead, but you'll just have to put on the same clothes again." Colin was standing by the window where the air conditioning was running, making the little curtain above it flutter with the movement.

"You're right," she muttered as she started to pace. Their clothes were dry and grungy. No sense in showering until they were back in New Orleans.

She couldn't even check her phone, couldn't reach out to anyone right now, and felt far too vulnerable. And she was hungry, something her stomach decided to announce to the room with a ridiculously loud growl.

Colin looked at her, eyes wide. "Was that you?"

She gave him a dry look.

"There were some pastries in the main office that actually looked good. I'll grab you some."

"No, it's fine. Let's just wait." She looked at the digital clock. "They'll be here soon." Only fifteen or so minutes to go.

"No one's driven up," he said, peeking out as another semi went by, given the rumble in the room. "I'll be fast." He grabbed a ball cap from his backpack and slid it on before he ducked outside.

Her stomach growled again.

"Hush up, you," she ordered herself, only to be met with more noise.

Sighing, she headed to the bathroom to take care of business while Colin was out. After washing her hands, she stepped back out and saw him already there, hunched over his backpack. "Hey—" Oh shit, that wasn't Colin.

She ducked back into the bathroom and slammed the door before turning the flimsy lock. Adrenaline surged through her as she leaned into the door, using her body weight to push back.

She jerked forward under a hit or kick from the other side.

"Open the damn door and things will go easier on you," the man growled. "We don't want to hurt you."

Yeah, right. Her stomach made a loud protest, clearly agreeing with her that he was a liar. "The cops are on their way, asshole!" she snarled. Where was Colin? Had they hurt him?

He laughed as if he knew she was lying, and the door shook under his weight again.

Since she was short, she propped her feet up on the little sink and pushed back. But everything had gone really quiet. And with this flimsy door the only thing protecting her at the moment, she couldn't hold him off forever.

Oh shit, was he going to shoot her? Because a bullet would tear through the cheap MDF door.

She eased down and stepped into the shower/bath combo as quietly as she could. The long, narrow window looked as if it had been painted over years ago, but maybe she could—

The man came flying through the bathroom door backward, hitting his head on the mirror. The glass cracked under the impact, shattering everywhere as he tried to push himself up.

Mari jumped, ready to attack him, but Colin was there, grabbing him by the shirt and dragging him back into the other room.

Mari rushed after them, looking for a weapon as Colin punched him in the face. This time, the guy sprawled backward onto the dirty carpet and stayed down.

She dove for her backpack, pulled out a bungee cord and tossed it to Colin before pulling out her flare gun, the only thing she had that could work as a weapon. She loaded the cartridge into the barrel as Colin rolled the man onto his back, started tying his hands.

Still crouching, Mari looked down the length of the barrel to check it just as the motel door burst open. A woman in dark boots holding a pistol strode in, expression hard.

Mari didn't even think as she aimed and pulled the trigger.

A whooshing sound exploded as the flare slammed into the woman. She stumbled back under the impact, dropping her pistol outside the room onto the sidewalk. And that was when her puffy jacket burst into flames. Screaming, the woman threw herself onto the ground and started rolling around, trying to put herself out.

"Come on." Colin grabbed his backpack as she slung hers over her shoulder and raced after him.

He scooped up the fallen pistol and tucked it into the back of his pants as they jumped over the flailing woman. As they ran across the parking lot, a man and woman who were sitting on the back of a truck drinking slushies stared at them, wide-eyed. (She also noticed they didn't make an effort to call anyone, like the cops.)

The woman's screaming faded as they ran the length of the motel to the front office. Mari was pretty sure they should call the cops at this point.

Or maybe... "That's what they were driving!" She pointed at the Land Rover. "Can you hot-wire a vehicle?" She actually could, but not something that new. Too many electronics and computer parts.

"No need, your friends are here."

Relief slammed into Mari so hard as a familiar SUV tore into the parking lot, tires squealing with the sharp turn.

She didn't think, just grabbed Colin's hand and ran for it.

The back door flew open to reveal Bradford already scooting over to make room.

"We were just attacked in our motel room," Mari managed to gasp out as they dove inside.

"Are your attackers down?" Berlin asked as she turned the vehicle.

"Yes, but they have that Land Rover."

"Hold on," Chance murmured. Berlin slowed, clearly knowing what he planned. He jumped out, shot out the two back tires and jumped back into the SUV in seconds.

"The motel didn't have any cameras outside that I saw," Colin said as Berlin tore onto the two-lane highway. "Just one at the check-in."

Now Mari could finally breathe. But she knew that they weren't out of the woods. Not by a long shot. Because whoever was after them was persistent.

And she was pretty sure that guy could have easily killed her if he'd wanted to. All he'd have had to do was shoot through the cheap motel door. She couldn't imagine why he'd want her alive—or why anyone wanted her dead for that matter.

But it was weird that he'd just tried to break into the bathroom instead of shooting through the door. "Did that guy say anything to you?" she murmured as she leaned her head on Colin's shoulder.

"No. I just saw him attacking the door and threw myself at him. Probably not the best tactical decision," he muttered, his arm around her protectively.

"It worked, didn't it? Thank you for saving my life...again." She repressed a shiver.

He didn't respond, simply wrapped his arm tighter around her shoulders. So she closed her eyes and leaned into him, feeling safe with him in a way she never had before.

CHAPTER 23

"I'm so glad you're okay." Camila rushed at Mari as soon as she, Colin and the others stepped into the safe house.

"You might not want to hug me," she said even as she gripped her friend tight. "I've been hiking through the woods."

"And apparently running from some gun toting assholes. I already talked to the sheriff up in the West Feliciana Parish and they picked up the two people who attacked you. One's in the ER." And Camila looked positively happy about that. But then she looked at Colin, her expression cooling a bit.

"He saved my life. Twice. We're gonna let old shit go, okay?" She looked at Colin, who just blinked between the two of them. "She knows what you said."

"I was a stupid kid—young man," he grumbled. "And I'm very sorry." Somehow he looked adorable as he apologized.

She turned back to Camila. "Who else is here?" she asked as Berlin, Chance and Bradford piled into the foyer.

"Just me. I figured you two would be exhausted and wouldn't need anyone else in your face."

"But the cops know that we were the victims?"

"Yes. I've already explained why you ran, that someone has been trying to kill you for days and that you didn't know who to trust. They're going to be contacting you, but we should be able to smooth things over so you can give a statement over Zoom."

Not to mention that Mari and Colin still needed to talk to NTSB, and soon, about the investigation into the flight "incident." They had to file their official report. Luckily since there was no actual damage to anyone or any property other than the plane being clearly sabotaged, it should be open and shut on their end. And Gary had airplane tow service so his insurance would have covered the towing.

"Oh, and I've got a phone you can use until you replace yours," Berlin added as they dumped their backpacks into the foyer. "But first, why don't you two shower and change and then we'll talk."

She looked up at Colin. "I'd rather get everything over with now and then shower. What about you?"

"Same." He hadn't said much on the drive back to New Orleans, but he was standing protectively close to her.

And she was glad for his presence. But she wasn't sure where things stood with them. Though with everything going on, that wasn't her top priority.

"Okay, come on." Camila turned and headed back to what turned out to be a kitchen.

They were in a different safe house than the one from before, and this one had a shotgun-style layout. The kitchen was in the center of the house and it looked like the bedrooms extended beyond.

Mari and Colin sat at the center island while Camila and Berlin stood across from them. Bradford and Chance disappeared into the back, likely to double-check things, if she had to guess.

"So what have you found?" Mari asked, fighting a yawn. She'd dozed a little on the drive back, but her body felt like it was shutting down from pure mental exhaustion. She'd been in flight mode and now that she knew they were safe (relatively speaking) she wanted to curl up and fall asleep next to Colin. And eat a lot of carbs.

"Ackerman is definitely shady. He's on the DEA's watchlist. And for the record, none of this leaves this room," Camila said.

Berlin scoffed.

"I know, I know, you know how to keep secrets, but I'm throwing it out there anyway. Also, the DEA can't locate Ackerman. But the DEA *has* linked him to some low-level cartel members—of the Suarez cartel. Apparently they suspect him of transporting drugs for them using his contacts from his day job. There recently became a bit of a vacuum out west when the Becerra cartel lost so many of their people and now it seems the Suarez one is looking to swoop in and take all their lost territory."

"So the DEA thinks he's really into drug smuggling?" She glanced at Colin. Apparently he'd been right about Ackerman. Still didn't explain people trying to kill them.

"Oh yeah," Camila said, with Berlin nodding next to her. "But the two people who tried to kill you are currently being questioned. And we're running their fingerprints. The DEA is hoping to find a connection between the suspected hired killers and Ackerman. They think once they have that, they might have enough to bring him in—once they locate him."

"What does that mean for us? For Mari?" Colin asked, his voice raspy. He had to be as tired as she was, but he certainly didn't look it.

"I want you both to sit tight. I know you need to file an official report with NTSB and do interviews and that's fine. But no flying, no nothing right now until we find Ackerman and figure out what the hell is going on. I've got friends with the DEA so they're not going to shut me out of this investigation." She glanced at her phone. "In fact, I'm pretty sure they've already taken over the interviewing of the two who tried to kill you. So you'll probably end up being interviewed by them instead."

Mari nodded, but didn't feel any better about the whole situation. "I need to call my clients and arrange other options for them." She occasionally worked with other contract pilots in situations like this. Her friends did favors for her and she did the same for them.

"One of my guys can take your flights for the next couple weeks," Colin murmured.

Surprised, she looked up at him. "Really?"

"We'll make it work."

"Thanks." She didn't want to put all the changes on his partner, but having an extra pilot in addition to the people she planned to reach out to would be a big help.

"And he won't try to steal your clients," he added, a grin tugging at his mouth.

His very kissable mouth that she needed to stop staring at. Things felt different now that they were back in New Orleans.

She looked back at Berlin. "Are we good to stay here for a while?"

"You could move in forever," Berlin said. "But it won't come to that, I'm sure. We've got clothes and toiletries for both of you in the back bedrooms."

"And that's my cue because I need to get home. Emma needs help with some theater stuff and I promised I'd be there. Mari, I love you and we're going to figure this out." Camila was walking around the island as she spoke. "I've got my phone on me 24/7 so call if you need anything."

Mari hugged her friend again before Berlin walked her out. Once they were alone—because Bradford and Chance had disappeared—she said, "Your guy really won't mind taking over my flights?"

"Nah. We've got a slow couple weeks anyway."

"I feel like you're lying."

His mouth curved up, making him look years younger. "I'm not."

"Okay, well, I've got another couple pilots I'll be reaching out to. Between them and your guy, I should have enough to cover all my clients and not piss anyone off."

"What about your main client?"

"Gary? He'll be fine. I fly him the majority of the year, but he's had fill-ins before when I'm on vacation or whatever." He'd been so loyal, moving with her when she'd struck out on her own. And he'd sent a decent amount of business her way.

"I thought you said his insurance wouldn't cover anyone else." His tone was dry.

She felt her cheeks heat up. "I might have been exaggerating."

Colin just snorted, but paused as Berlin strode back in.

"Okay now that Camila is gone, we can talk about our plan."

Mari blinked. "Plan?"

"Yep. I trust the DEA just fine, but we're not leaving this completely in their hands. We need to figure out why Ackerman wants you dead and then figure out a way to make him stop. Or stop him. If we can get him on video doing illegal shit, he'll be locked up and that should hopefully end your problem with him."

"And if that doesn't work?" Colin asked.

"Then we'll stop him another way." Berlin's expression was slightly feral as she answered.

Mari was glad that Berlin was on her side and she definitely wasn't against stopping Ackerman "another way." She wasn't going to let someone destroy her life without standing up to him.

"Oh, also," Berlin continued, "Magnolia has been blowing up my phone so please call your girl and let her know that you're okay. All your previous numbers are programmed into that phone."

"You're an angel, thank you. I'll probably shower too after calling her." She looked at Colin. "You good?"

"Are you worried about leaving him with me?" Now Berlin looked amused.

"Of course not, but be nice." She gave her friend a pointed look.

"I'm fine." Colin's tone was dry. "And also kinda hungry. I think I've had enough protein bars for a lifetime."

No kidding.

Berlin was telling him all about the food in the fridge as Mari headed to the back where she found Bradford and Chance talking quietly in the farthest bedroom.

"Everything good?" There were clothes that looked like they'd fit her on the bed so it was a good guess that this was her room.

"Yep. House is secure," Bradford said. "We just didn't want to overwhelm you."

"I'm fine, I promise. Just make sure Berlin is nice to Colin."

Chance just chuckled as they strode out. "There's no controlling that woman."

Yeah, that was accurate.

Bradford gave her a kiss on the side of her head and a half hug before heading out. Once she was alone, Mari collapsed on the tufted chair by the window and called her best friend.

"Mari, you're okay!" Magnolia said by way of answering.

And that was when the tears fell. Because hearing her best friend's voice was everything.

CHAPTER 24

When in doubt, hold on to your altitude. No one has ever collided with the sky.

"I'm pretty sure we've gotten everyone covered." Mari looked at the schedule she and Colin had come up with.

After two hours of calling and texting with his partners and her pilot friends, she had all her upcoming flights covered for the next three weeks. She hadn't wanted to go that deep into her schedule but was glad Colin had pushed her to extend it. It was easier to schedule now than scramble to find replacements later.

She just hoped it wasn't necessary. "The only person I haven't heard back from is Gary but—" She laughed as her phone rang and saw his name on screen.

"Kinda late for him to be calling," Colin muttered.

She blinked at his weird tone, but scooped up her phone and headed into the back bedroom. She'd already scheduled Gary with one of her favorite people, Summer, another pilot she'd worked with numerous times over the years. "Hey, you didn't have to call me back so late," she said as she shut the bedroom door behind her. She'd already showered and changed into the pajamas that Berlin had provided and was seriously considering passing out on the giant fluffy bed soon.

"I know but I'm up anyway. Working on some bullshit." And he sounded frustrated by it. Though to be fair, he always sounded frustrated with his job. "I saw the time stamp and figured it was okay to call. And yes, Summer is a great choice if you're not available. But is everything okay?"

"Yeah, just a family emergency. Not sure how long it'll take so I'm scheduling out a few weeks in case I end up needing her."

"Okay. That works for me, but you know you're my number one."

She grinned as she sat on the edge of the bed. "That's right. Listen...I have a question and it's okay if you can't answer. Things didn't work out with your friend Ackerman and me." She wanted to see if Gary knew where Ackerman was and pass on the information to Camila, but wanted to be smooth about it.

Gary snorted softly. "Not surprised. He's been pissing off a lot of people this week, myself included."

"Really?" She didn't talk to him much about his work. In the beginning he'd talked about it, but it was probably as boring as her talking aviation to him would be. For the most part, she listened, but didn't retain any of it.

"Yep. He missed a meeting with me and two others I know of. Did he blow you off? Because he blew off one of his normal pilots and has been MIA since."

"Is that typical for him?" Mari figured she'd get all the information she could on Ackerman and pass it on to Camila or maybe even the DEA.

He paused so long she checked her phone screen to make sure they hadn't disconnected.

"You okay?" she asked.

He shoved out a sigh. "Yeah. Between us, he sometimes dabbles in drugs. Cocaine mostly. Not in recent years, but in the past he went on a couple benders and each time disappeared for days at a time. Once for almost two weeks. But he's been in rehab and sober for a while. I really thought his sobriety had stuck this time. And I know he's got a personality that rubs people the wrong way, but...if I'm being honest, I'm a little worried about him. I guess it's easier to be angry that he blew me off but I'm worried it might be something else."

"I'm really sorry." Mari didn't have anything else to offer, especially not when she was pretty sure Ackerman wanted her dead.

But the cocaine thing was interesting, and was something she would pass on to Berlin immediately. Maybe Berlin could figure out who his dealer was? *Ugh.* Mari wasn't even sure if that would matter. She liked flying planes, not solving crimes.

"Thanks. Listen, I know it's late. I just wanted to check in and let you know everything is good on my end. And whenever you're ready to fly me again, I'm here. But if you need anything, let me know."

"I will, thanks." After disconnecting, she stared at the bedroom door, wondering if she should go back out there and talk to Colin.

Or maybe she could be a big coward and just go to bed without saying anything else to him. They'd figured out the schedule and it was now almost midnight. She was tired, and didn't want to remotely think about things between them.

Not after they'd both gotten each other off, then run from bad guys, gotten attacked by bad guys, and were now in a safe house hiding out. What the hell had her life become?

She made it to the door, ready to go out there and talk to him, but as she started to turn the knob she knew that they would be doing more than talking. And she desperately wanted that—which scared the hell out of her. She was starting to fall for him in a way she'd never imagined. He'd gotten under her skin, had saved her life (twice), and now she knew what he looked like naked, what he looked like climaxing... She let her hand drop and decided the coward's way out was best. She turned off the light and slid beneath the covers. Tomorrow she'd deal with her stupid emotions and whatever was going on with her and Colin.

After texting Berlin and Camila about what Gary had told her about Ackerman, she shot Colin a quick text to tell him that she was crashing. *Coward, coward, coward.*

Then she closed her eyes, and to her surprise, sleep wasn't far behind.

CHAPTER 25

Maybe it won't work out, but maybe it will—and just maybe it will be the greatest adventure of your life.

"Mari?" Colin called out as he stepped into the bathroom. The shower was running so he knew she was in there. Thankfully she hadn't locked the door—not that a flimsy lock would have stopped him at this point.

And yeah, he knew he was acting crazy, but he didn't care. After her text last night, he was on a razor's edge of control. Things had changed between them and there was no way she could deny her attraction to him. But it was more than that—there was something real between them. A spark he'd never once experienced with someone else. This was the kind of thing that was real, could grow into something forever.

The curtain pulled back to reveal Mari with suds in her jet-black hair, eyes wide as she stared at him. "What are you doing, you psycho? You're just barging in here!"

"I'd rather be a psycho than a coward!"

She glared at him, her dark eyes narrowing. "I have no idea what you're talking about!"

"Liar."

"Excuse me?"

"You're *lying*. You disappeared last night without a word, then sent that stupid text. What the hell Mari," he growled.

"Yeah, because I was tired. I told you." Her voice was defensive, but he could see something else in her eyes.

"Bullshit. You're a coward. You didn't want to talk about us."

"There is no us."

"Oh really? So we didn't make each other come behind that waterfall? Didn't fall asleep in each other's arms? Didn't run for our lives together and put the past behind us?"

"Oh my god. I don't want to talk about this. Things were weird, we were both feeling all sorts of emotions and stuff happened. It's not like we ever have to talk about it again. I'm fine pretending that the waterfall incident never happened."

"Well I'm not." He leaned against the doorframe, watching her intently. "And I want more."

She held his gaze for a long, charged moment, conflicting emotions flickering across her face. "Just sex? No running back to my brother and telling him about this?"

"Mari, I promise you, your *brother* isn't on my mind right now." But no way was he promising that this was just about sex. She could deny it all she wanted, but there was something real between them, if only she took a chance.

"Fine." She yanked the curtain back and he forgot to breathe at the sight of her wet, gloriously naked body, even if she was still clearly pissed at him.

Apparently he liked a pissed-off Mari. Or Mari in any way he could get her. And now he'd learned something else about her: she was going to run from him so he couldn't let her retreat. He should have talked to her last night, instead of bottling everything up.

He moved fast, stripping off his shirt and lounge pants before stepping into the shower with her. The water pounded down around her, rinsing out the shampoo from her hair as she still glared up at him.

She set one hand on her hip. "This is just sex—"

He crushed his mouth to hers, murmured, "Please shut up," as he nipped her bottom lip.

She gave a sort of indignant yelp but leaned into him, wrapping her arms around his body so they were completely skin-to-skin and holding on to him as if she never wanted to let go.

Which was just fine with him, because he wasn't letting this woman go. Ever. Unfortunately, he had a lot of time to make up for. He never should have said that bullshit years ago, never should have let the chasm between them grow even when he didn't know why she was angry.

He'd always been a little intimidated by her, still was. But he knew her and understood that she was trying to put up walls by making this just about sex. He could let her pretend this was purely physical. For now.

"Oh god," she moaned as he slid a hand between her legs, cupped her mound, began teasing her clit.

He loved the way she rolled her hips against him, in a slow, sensuous rhythm as he pleasured her. As he teased her, she reached between their bodies and grasped onto his hard length.

And god help him, he loved the feel of her fingers wrapping around him, stroking— *No.* He eased back, his jaw tight as he placed his other hand over hers. "Not yet," he managed to rasp out, not missing the mischievous gleam in her eyes as she looked up at him.

She was intensely gorgeous like this, with the sunlight streaming in from the high window, all slick and natural and...he was past the point of no return with her. It was a sobering realization. Also... "I don't have a condom."

"Me neither, damn it...but I'm on the pill and clean. It's been a minute since I've been with anyone."

Yeah, it had been a minute for him too. Minute, years, same difference. "I'm clean too." They were tested regularly in the military and he hadn't been with anyone since his last test. Starting a new business had taken up all of his waking hours, and the truth was, being back in the same city with Mari had lit something on fire inside him. He'd been fighting his feelings for her for too long.

"Normally I wouldn't take someone at their word, but I trust you."

Something about those words speared right through to the heart of him. "I trust you too." Because no matter what, Mari Kim wasn't a liar.

She leaned up right as he leaned down and claimed her mouth. But the kisses weren't enough. Nothing was enough with this woman who had him so wound up he could never think straight around her. He always felt on edge, as if he was constantly about to fall over a waterfall.

And they were about to have sex without a condom? No barriers between him and the woman he'd fallen for ages ago. This was heaven.

Not that he could tell her about his deeper feelings. No way. If he admitted the intensity of them, she would run. Kinda like she had last night.

So he kissed her and teased between her legs until she was so close she was shaking from almost coming. Then he lifted her up against him, savored the way she wrapped her toned legs around him as he slowly slid inside her, inch by inch.

She sucked in a breath as he pressed her up against the wall, taking all of him as she dug her heels into his ass.

The way her inner walls tightened around him, clenched with need as he pulled out then pushed in again, almost sent him over the edge right then and there.

Almost.

Because she was definitely coming first.

As he began thrusting inside her she met him stroke for stroke. He held back his own release even though his body was desperate, his control on a slippery slope.

But when he reached between their bodies and began teasing that little bundle of nerves, she arched into him, her inner walls tightening faster and faster. Oh, she was close.

When she bit his bottom lip, dug her fingernails into his back, he knew it wouldn't be long. Then she was coming around him, crying out his name, and he finally allowed himself to let go.

"Mari." He groaned out her name as he found his own release, holding on to her and hoping he didn't leave marks—or maybe he wanted to. Because god knew he wanted her to remember the feel of him inside her, on her. Claiming her.

Because this woman had completely claimed him, even if she didn't realize it yet.

Chapter 26

Life is simple: eat, sleep, fly.

Mari cuddled into Colin, not wanting to move after spending the last few hours in bed with him—some sleeping because they definitely needed it. She kept trying to convince herself that this was all about sex but it was hard to lie to herself.

"So have you spent a lot of time with Bear since being back?" she murmured, enjoying the quiet. They could hear some outside noises of the city but the place was well insulated because it wasn't much.

"I don't want to talk about another man while we're in bed naked." His tone was dry, but there was an underlying edge that surprised her.

She pinched his side. "Bear isn't a man. He's your brother...and one of the nicest people I know."

"Hey, I'm nice."

She snorted.

"Not sure if I should be insulted," he murmured as he pulled her closer so that she was splayed up against him. She loved all the skin-to-skin with him. "But yes, we get together for lunch at least twice a week. I've taken Valentine up a few times to view the city and now she's talking about learning to fly. But Bear is still okay being on the ground."

"I never understood how a big guy like him is so scared of flying."

"He says it's *because* he's so big. He's worried about crashing the plane."

Mari barked out a laugh. "Apparently we need to explain center of gravity and balance to him."

"I've tried. And I know he understands it, but..." He shrugged. "He says if Valentine gets her PPL he'll go in the air with her. Not his *brother*, who's been a pilot forever."

She snickered as she stretched. "Sounds about right. My halmeoni goes up with me all the time. And my dad does sometimes too."

"Your grandma and not your mom?"

"She always says she doesn't have time, but...I think she's secretly scared."

"Maybe she and Bear can start a club. The big baby club."

Surprised at his tone, she looked up at him. "Are you mad at Bear?"

"No. Not exactly. Look, I get fears, but I'm his brother, he should trust me." Colin sounded indignant.

"Oh my god, *right*?" Laughing, she laid her head back down on his chest. "Or we're just assholes who aren't very understanding. Flying is the best thing in the world. Being up in the air, everything else seems so trivial. Though to be fair, I wouldn't be mad at Bear because he's perfect— Hey, did you just pinch me?"

"It's your butt, it doesn't count. And Bear is not perfect. He snores. And he's not great at parallel parking," Colin growled.

"I don't even know what you're talking about at this point. Are those supposed to be good examples of..." She looked up at him again, pushing up against the sheets in surprise. "Wait, are you being jealous?"

"No. Maybe. I don't like you saying Bear is perfect. How would you feel if I said Carmen was perfect?"

"Uh, I'd *agree* with you because she married my dumbass brother. She's a saint for putting up with him and we should build an altar to her or whatever people do for saints. Plus she cooks for me all the time so I think that ranks her at goddess status."

"You're ridiculous." But his mouth was curving up in amusement.

"You like it," she murmured.

"I do like it." His gaze fell to her mouth, and just like that, heat curled in her belly.

And since her body was determined to betray her, her stomach growled again. Loudly.

Which made him throw his head back and full-on laugh. "Apparently I'm not feeding you enough. Come on. Berlin left us a ton to choose from."

Though she was reluctant to leave the bed, she followed after him in search of food, not bothering with clothes. Hopefully they could head right back to the bedroom after they were done eating.

She knew this wasn't going to last, that this whole thing between them was because of the situation they were in. But she was going to take advantage of it because Colin was literally the man of her fantasies.

So she would enjoy this until she had to return to her normal life. Because he might say he wanted more than sex, but he was best friends with her brother. And fine, she was just making excuses. She didn't know how to do relationships.

To be fair, she'd never really tried, but what happened if she did try, if she gave this her everything and then still failed? She'd have lost the best man she'd ever known and wrecked a relationship between Evan and Colin. That was a lot of pressure, and ugh, she was spiraling.

Forcing her thoughts on better things, she focused on the present—and Colin's perfect ass as he headed toward the kitchen.

CHAPTER 27

"You're good to go," Cash said over the phone line.

Cash, aka Constantine Pierce, worked out of Redemption Harbor Security's North Carolina office. The same one Bradford had worked out of for a couple years. And everything the man touched turned to gold. Or cash, as it was, hence the nickname. But he didn't just hoard it away like a greedy dragon; he gave to more charities and scholarships than Bradford had even known existed. He'd completely changed the landscape and future of a handful of small towns around the country.

"Really?" Bradford asked. He'd called the Colorado aviation company that Ackerman flew with most of the time and tried to get an appointment to simply talk to someone. And he'd been rejected. Twice.

"Yep. Told them that you're a friend of mine and wanted to go over specifics about a new contract. They said no problem."

"Money really talks," he murmured. Knowing it was one thing, but it still amazed him sometimes to see it so blatantly in action.

"No kidding. The woman I spoke to was an asshole though, for the record. I don't think she wanted to agree to the appointment, but someone must have flagged my name. The appointment is this afternoon. You've got an hour to be there."

Yeah, that wasn't a surprise. When someone like Constantine Pierce called, people listened. "Thanks. We're not even sure if this will matter but Berlin wants me to talk to them in person, get a feel for their operations. Maybe hack into their systems." With Berlin, you never knew.

"And what Berlin wants, she gets," he said with a laugh. "How are things going with this case?"

It wasn't an official case, but Bradford knew what he meant. "Confusing, mostly. Someone is trying to kill Mari. Or scare her. Though at this point I'm pretty sure it's kill, considering the two people with guns in her motel room. And we still haven't figured out why."

"And you can't find this Ackerman guy?"

"No, but we're working on it. I'm going to mention him at the appointment today, then Berlin has an idea."

"Does that idea involve explosives?"

"I really hope not." Or maybe that wouldn't be a bad idea. Only time would tell. Sometimes blowing shit up really was the answer to everything.

***

"How's the connection?" Bradford murmured as he pulled into the parking lot of Five C's Aviation. He was undercover, using one of the many fake IDs that Berlin had created for everyone, including a bit of stage makeup to change the shape of his nose, ears and jawline.

He preferred more basic covers, but understood why sometimes they had to use deeper ones. They had no idea who really ran this aviation company—there were too many LLCs to sift through to figure out the original owner, and they were under investigation by the DEA, which told him all he needed to know. So he couldn't walk in with his normal face even with a fake ID. Because if they were really some cartel or a similar criminal organization, they'd be able to run his face and figure out who he was later.

"Loud and clear," Berlin said into his earpiece. "I see and hear what you do. And if anything goes sideways, we've got your six."

He knew that they did. Berlin, Chance, Adalyn and Ezra were waiting in an SUV a mile down the road. He'd had to drive into Biloxi since it was the closest location of one of their satellite offices and the company was about to close. According to the website, the actual airport was open 24/7, but the main office shut down at five. Which seemed early for an airport.

But he'd made it right before four and just in time for his appointment.

Once inside, he was blasted with the icy artificial air that must be turned down to sixty-five. He smiled at the woman behind the counter, a redhead with ivory skin and a deadpan expression. "How may I help you?" Even her voice was expressionless.

"My name is Reginald Overby and I'm here for an appointment with Blanca Stein." Seriously, where did Berlin come up with these names? Reginald Overby? He sounded like some snooty British guy.

She looked at the sleek computer in front of her and simply nodded at him. "This way, please."

He'd been in enough private airports over the years, first with the Marines and then once he started working with Redemption Harbor Security, and this was one of the nicest. Normally the airports he'd been flown into had been under the cover of night in planes with blacked-out windows and no one had known he and his team had been there.

Everything was all sleek marble and chrome, something he wouldn't have known from outside. On the outside it looked like a giant warehouse.

She opened a glass office door for him, then left without another word. Just to be a dick, he said, "If you've got sparkling water, I'd love some."

She gave him a tight smile—or what might be classified as a smile—and nodded at him. "Of course, sir." The *sir* dripped with disdain.

The woman behind the desk stood, with a much warmer smile, and motioned for him to sit. "Mr. Overby, I'm Blanca and it's lovely to meet you. But first, let me apologize for our receptionist. She's related to the owner and unfortunately I can't fire her."

Bradford blinked at her blunt honesty, then laughed. "I thought maybe I'd done something to piss her off." According to his background, he was from Georgia, so he leaned into his accent. There were some fun things about being undercover, and becoming someone else was one of them. Most days he just wished he could be someone that his wife wanted to stick around for.

"The world at large pisses her off." Blanca's tone was dry, but there was a slight edge to her words.

And something told Bradford that the receptionist might end up fired after all.

"But at least she is good for some things, like fetching." Her words were coated in ice as the woman delivered his drink.

Bradford couldn't miss the tight clench of the receptionist's jaw or the angry glare she shot Blanca.

Okay, so this was just plain weird and uncomfortable. "Thank you," he murmured, taking the drink, wondering if he should actually drink it. It actually seemed plausible that she'd put something in it. He set it on the glass table next to him and smiled pleasantly at the woman across from him.

She had dark hair, skin as pale as the woman out front, and while her smile was pleasant, her eyes were flecks of ice. It was a strange combination. "So what can I do for you today?"

"I'm interested in diversifying who I work with. Right now I use

WILCO Aviation for work and pleasure, but I've been with them for so long I thought it wouldn't hurt to shop around."

"And you're doing this personally?" She arched a perfect eyebrow.

"Since I'm the one who'll be flown around, yes." He laid on his accent a little thicker. "I was raised to do some things myself and I like to know who will be flying me. I need to trust my pilot."

She gave him a faint smile. "The company you work with is a solid one with a good reputation. And I'm afraid you'll find our rates are quite a bit higher than theirs, so you won't be saving money if that is your intent."

That wasn't true, something he knew from Berlin's research.

He barked out a laugh. "Well I do appreciate your honesty. So no deals for new customers?"

She gave him the same faint smile as before. "No. My boss doesn't believe in discounts. And if I'm being transparent, I took this meeting because of Mr. Constantine Pierce. We've been hoping to snag him as a client for years."

Bradford nodded, glancing around the office curiously—and also so Berlin would be able to see everything he did, thanks to his glasses. "I understand that. The man's got enough money to burn a wet mule."

She blinked at him. "I've never heard that expression before."

He just chuckled politely. "Something my daddy used to say. Well, I do appreciate your honesty and taking the time to meet with me. Even if things aren't going to work out between us, would it be too much to ask for a tour of this place? It's one of the nicer private airports I've been in."

She gave him a real smile then. "Thank you. I actually designed this place," she said, pride in her voice as she stood. "I'll give you a quick tour."

The tour was only twenty minutes, but he made sure to look at everything they passed. He didn't think it would give them much in the way of finding Ackerman, but there was a chance Berlin had been able to hack into

Blanca's computer or cell phone since he'd been near them both. Though he wouldn't know until he got out to the SUV.

Once they were done touring the office and the two hangars, she walked him out to the parking lot, her steps a little more brisk than before.

"Thank you," he said, shaking her hand. "You've got a great place here. And I promise to pass on how kind you've been to Cash. Maybe you'll get him as a client one day."

He got another small smile. This one looked real too. "I appreciate that. And I'm sorry we couldn't accommodate you." She looked over her shoulder at the airport and it seemed like her gaze flicked up to one of the cameras, but he couldn't be sure. Then she turned back to him. "Right now we're booked solid with new clients and our pilots' schedules are completely full. A good problem to have, I know. But I'm going to save your information and hopefully in the future we might get to work with each other."

"Thank you kindly." He shook her hand before heading to the SUV. "So what did you think?" he asked Berlin as he shut the door behind him. The windows were tinted so no one would see him talking.

"That she's going to do a deeper dive into you and see if you're legit. From what I can tell, whoever actually owns the company has some clients with legal businesses and some who are suspected to be dealing in illegal things. Namely drugs and weapons. If they want to keep their portfolio diversified—and to make it harder for the Feds to pin shit on them—they might want to expand their clients with legal business interests."

"The exchange between Blanca and the receptionist was weird though, right?"

"Oh yeah, and very interesting. I'm running the receptionist's face to see if I can get a hit. If Blanca was telling the truth about not being able to fire her, this might lead us to someone else."

"Definitely... *If* Blanca was telling the truth," he tacked on. And he hadn't been able to tell. He was relatively good at reading people. He'd had to be, to survive, but the woman's eyes had been...off, for lack of a better description.

"Agreed. So what does this mean for Mari?"

"Nothing yet," Berlin said.

Then Adalyn came over the comm line. "You up for another trip tonight?"

"Of course. Where to?" Anything to keep his mind off his estranged wife. Where she was and if she was in danger.

"We're going to go back to the source of all that shit. That little airport where Mari took Ackerman the first time. She said there were a couple cameras outside but no huge security presence. So we're going to fly in close to there, then drive in and see if Berlin can hack—"

"I can definitely hack whatever they've got," Berlin cut in, clearly insulted.

"Yeah you can," Bradford added.

"That's why you're my favorite." He could hear her smile through the line.

"Suck up," Adalyn muttered, but he heard the laughter in her voice. "Head to the airport. We'll leave directly from there."

They'd flown into a small airport in Ocean Springs, then driven over to Biloxi. "What about Mari? She'll be pissed if we leave her behind." Though Camila would be pissed if they took her.

"We're picking up her and Colin on the way," Adalyn said.

"I don't know what I think about that Colin," Berlin added.

"I like the guy." Bradford hadn't been sure at first, but the man looked at Mari like she hung the moon.

"Me too," Chance chimed in.

Adalyn just grunted, which could mean anything. Then she said, “Okay, enough of this shit. We’ll see you at the airport. If you think you have a tail—”

“I know. I’ll just head out on a different flight.” On the off chance he was followed as Reginald Overby, he wasn’t going to lead anyone back to his crew. No way in hell.

They were his family in a way his biological family had never been.

CHAPTER 28

"You two aren't coming with us." There was no give in Adalyn's voice as they reached the two rental vehicles.

Mari was grateful that the Redemption Harbor Security crew had picked up her and Colin for the flight to the hangar where she'd had that weird interaction with Ackerman. Well, they hadn't taken them to the actual hangar, but another airport about half an hour away. Then they'd rented two vehicles under one of their cover IDs and the RHS crew was going to drive to the hangar and do their thing. Meanwhile, she and Colin were just supposed to sit tight and do nothing.

Which Mari hated. Sure, she wasn't trained like the others, something she understood and appreciated. But sitting around wasn't her style.

"Then why'd you even bring us?" Mari leaned against the dark SUV, Colin right next to her.

"We could be assets. Park down the road, be extra eyes for backup," Colin added. "I saw the drone you packed."

Adalyn looked between the two of them, raised an eyebrow. Then she looked at the others and they seemed to have a silent conversation before Adalyn turned back to them. "Fine. You can follow, but you'll have to remain out of sight a couple miles back and fly the drone from there. Battery life is about forty-five minutes for the one we brought."

"There's a little turnoff for sightseeing about three quarters of a mile from the airport," Mari said. She'd been to this airport and about half of the smaller ones in Louisiana over the years. "We could park there."

It was clear that Adalyn was the official boss of everyone, even though she looked to her crew for their opinions. So Mari was being cautious around her. She and Berlin were friends, and while she thought of Adalyn as a friend, she also knew that the woman didn't take shit from anyone and would bring down the hammer if she thought it necessary.

"You two will not get out of the SUV except to launch the drone. I know you're both skilled with them, you especially," she said, looking at Colin, "but you're just here to be extra eyes for us."

"Ha, so you did bring us for a reason." Mari grinned, unable to stop herself. "You planned this and now you're acting like you're doing us a favor. You wanted one of us to fly the drone."

Adalyn's expression was dry as she eyed Mari, but her lips twitched. "Don't get cocky."

"That's like asking the sun not to shine," Colin murmured.

"Hey!"

"I didn't say it was a bad thing. I like your confidence." His voice dropped a couple octaves.

Oh. Oh, this was weird and now everyone was watching them. "We'll follow you guys," Mari muttered before she jumped into the SUV.

Colin got in the passenger side as she started the engine. "What just happened? Did I say something?"

"No." She watched as Chance got in the driver's seat of the other SUV and the rest of the team all slid in with military-type precision. They moved like a unit, like a team clearly used to working together. And she was glad they were on her side.

"Liar."

She glared at Colin before facing forward and pulling out of the parking lot of the little rental place next to the airport. "Call me a liar again and see what happens." She hadn't minded so much before because he'd been right and they'd ended up having incredible sex.

God, so many orgasms. She'd forgive a lot for that.

"Fine, but what just happened? You got all weird when I complimented you."

"I don't know. I just don't want anyone to know...about, well, whatever is going on between us. I like to keep my private life private. No one needs to know who I'm banging."

"Did you just say...banging?"

"Poor word choice. But you know what I mean."

"Please enlighten me." His voice had taken on a tone she'd never heard before and she definitely didn't like it.

"I just mean I don't want everyone to know we're sleeping together. Our business is our business. No one else's."

He went silent and that was more unnerving than him busting in on her when she'd been in the shower, all indignant over her trying to blow him off by text. At least then she'd known what he was thinking. She should have just had a conversation with him. Now...she didn't like this quiet, broody Colin at all.

She cleared her throat, trying to find any semblance of words that didn't sound stupid. "So you have a lot of experience with drones?" she asked as they turned onto the small two-lane highway with mostly swamp and marsh on either side of them.

"Yep."

She gritted her teeth at his one-word answer, even as she acknowledged that he *might* have a right to be frustrated. But she wasn't feeling super logical right now. Her emotions were all over the place and it was his fault. He'd barged into her life and was all wonderful and giving and this was new territory for her. "Is that what I can expect, one-word answers from you today?"

"I'm surprised you want more from someone who is clearly just your friend with benefits." Oh, that tone again.

"That's not what I said!"

"You implied it."

"No, I didn't. I simply said I didn't want everyone up in our business."

"Are you embarrassed about me?" he demanded.

"What? No. Don't be ridiculous."

"I'm not being ridiculous." His voice was heated now. Only a few lights guided them as she drove, the darkness out here eerie.

It was so damn dark out here at night, making everything seem eerier. "You're right, you're not ridiculous. I just meant I'm not embarrassed. I just like to keep my private life private, that's all. Sorry, I freaked out."

He was silent for a long moment, then spoke again. "So...what are we?"

"What do you mean?" She knew exactly what he meant but wanted to delay this conversation—or not have it at all. She slowed as she neared the turnoff for sightseeing, watched as the other SUV continued heading toward the airport in the distance, their lights a bright beacon illuminating the way. Though she was certain they'd cut them the closer they got to the other airport.

"I'd like to take you on a date once all this is over. See where this thing might go." His voice was strained and so unlike him.

She couldn't look at him as she parked because eye contact would do her in. She cleared her throat, trying to find the right words even though she didn't want to discuss this at all. "Can we talk about this later? Once we're not acting as backup for the people helping us stay alive?" she asked as she put the SUV in park.

"Sure."

Oh, she did not like that tone either, but there was nothing to do about it. He slid from the vehicle and popped the hatch to get the drone.

Crickets or cicadas chirped loudly, the sound filling the quiet of the vehicle before he shut the hatchback. Then moments later once he'd launched it, he slid back into the passenger seat, controller in hand.

There was a screen built into the middle of the controller and the night vision was stellar. As he guided it in the direction of the nearby airport, she was quiet, letting him work as she replayed their conversation and wondered what the hell was wrong with her.

She knew she was sabotaging this, but was so afraid of screwing up she couldn't figure out the right thing to say. Or do. God, why was this stuff so easy for some people?

Aviation, she understood. People...were so complicated.

CHAPTER 29

"Everyone in position?" Adalyn's voice came over the comm line quietly.

Bradford was twenty yards from the actual hangar, while Chance, Ezra and Adalyn were all in similar positions surrounding it. The airport itself was quiet, with the runway lights off. And Berlin had tapped into the radio frequency used for this non-towered airport just in case they had any unexpected visitors.

"Affirmative," he responded as the others did, sliding on his NVGs and clicking on the IR illuminator.

Then Berlin came over the comm line. "I've taken over the cameras. They're on a loop now but it's possible someone might realize a ghost is in the system. This is a higher-tech security system than I've ever seen at a small place like this. So far I haven't had any pushback but I want everyone to be aware."

"Going in," Bradford said, since he was assigned to breach the door. Though breach was probably the wrong word since they weren't using explosives. This time. Instead, at the door he slapped a device Berlin and a man named Gage—one of their founders—had created to break the security code.

Fifteen seconds and the lock face turned green. After a short beep of approval, they were in.

Weapon up, he eased the steel door open but remained half behind it in case this was a trap. "I'm in," he whispered.

He moved inside whisper quiet, pistol up as he swept the place. Thanks to the IR illuminator, he had enough light to make out the outline of multiple planes and... "I see a body." And no heat signature.

He felt, more than heard the others moving up behind him. "Fan out, look for more signs of life," Adalyn ordered.

They swept through the place as quickly as possible, having done this countless times together and in previous careers. In less than ten minutes they reconvened back at the front of the hangar, took off their NVGs, and Bradford hit the lights.

They flickered on with a whine, illuminating the expansive hangar to reveal a few vintage-looking planes and two very expensive Cessnas. Nothing out of the ordinary for an airport hangar.

Except Jeremy Ackerman's dead body right by the first plane. Wearing only boxer briefs and a thin white undershirt, he was covered in burn marks and bruises. But his face was mostly untouched and Bradford recognized him from the pictures.

"He's been tortured," Adalyn said as she leaned down next to him, took pictures. Because it was clear that he was long gone and had been for a while.

"A pro did this. For information." Bradford had moved up next to her, pointed at the burn marks in various places along his arms, his chest and on his legs. "I'm guessing a cartel."

"We need to get out of here and report this." Adalyn motioned to everyone as she stood.

And as a unit, they all moved at her order, leaving as quietly as they'd come. Because she was right. They had to report this. To Camila he guessed—anonymously—then she'd report it to the correct authorities here. DEA or FBI. Because there was no way they could report this themselves.

Nope.

They'd flown in under the cover of night on a plane not linked to their organization, rented two vehicles under cover IDs—and Berlin had already looped the security feeds so there was no evidence of them arriving or leaving. This couldn't come back on them.

And no one could know that Mari was involved in finding Ackerman at all. They'd gone to a lot of trouble staying off the radar of anyone and everyone that might be a threat to their company—and their families and loved ones—and that included cartels. Hell, especially cartels. Because if someone got a whiff that any one of them was going up against a cartel in any way, Redemption Harbor Security would find themselves in a war with brutal enemies.

He, Adalyn, Berlin, and Ezra headed out minutes later as quietly as they'd arrived and kept their balaclavas on until they were miles away, Mari and Colin trailing after them in the other SUV.

At least they hadn't seen anything suspicious on the drone so it appeared as if they were clear. Though he did find it odd that Ackerman's body had just been left there instead of buried. Or fed to gators. Whatever it was cartels did to their enemies' bodies.

But that was something to worry about once they were back in New Orleans.

CHAPTER 30

At a short knock on the bedroom door, Mari opened it and found Adalyn on the other side. It had been roughly twenty-four hours since they'd found Jeremy Ackerman's dead body, then "anonymously" reported it to Camila in the hopes she'd know who to report it to without involving them.

Mari had been back in the safe house along with Colin, Adalyn and Bradford. The others had gone home but they'd wanted to stay to keep an eye on them, which Mari appreciated.

What she didn't appreciate was Colin's weirdness.

Even if it was justified.

Damn it, she just hated everything about this situation. She wasn't good at relationships. Hell, her longest relationship had been with her private plane. The basic love of her life. Jesus, that was sad. And a little awesome, because that plane had taken her to places she'd always dreamed of.

"Everything okay?" She'd retreated to the bedroom an hour ago after having dinner with Adalyn in the kitchen.

"Camila's here."

Her heart jumped in her chest and she fell in step with Adalyn as they headed to the front of the house.

Colin was already sitting in the living room, his expression annoyingly neutral as his gaze fell on her. She looked away from him because she couldn't handle anything else right now.

Camila, who was always so put together, actually looked exhausted for the first time, but she smiled as Mari stepped into the room. "Hey, you get some rest?"

"I'm fine." She nodded, even though she hadn't because who cared. Her friends had been working around the clock, clearly giving up their own sleep to figure out what was going on and why someone wanted to kill her. "So...good news?"

"Sort of. Or it's heading that way. I called in a favor, managed to make an 'anonymous' tip about Ackerman's body. Now the DEA has taken over the case of his murder and gotten the warrants they needed. Not just because of the murder, but him being killed 'cartel-style' certainly didn't hurt. No one knows who found the body or who reported it. So even if there's a leak in any paperwork, that stuff simply isn't documented anywhere. Everyone here is covered."

Some of the tension in Mari's chest loosened. Knowing that this crap couldn't come back on her friends meant a lot.

"What does that mean for Mari and me?" Colin asked, his delicious rumbly voice wrapping around her.

"Right now you're still in a waiting pattern. I'm sorry, but I think it's best if you both sit tight and don't contact the outside world. The DEA is moving fast on this because of the war between the Becerra cartel and the Suarez cartel. They want to know why Ackerman was tortured, and the current belief is that he took something he shouldn't have. They're interviewing his wife right now."

"Thank you for all you're doing," Mari said, with Colin murmuring the same.

This wasn't what she'd wanted to hear but it wasn't terrible either. And it had only been a day. Barely twenty-four hours at that. They would just have to be patient, something she wasn't normally good at.

But at least she could see a light at the end of the tunnel. She and Colin could go back to their real lives.

CHAPTER 31

Two days later

Mari was about to go out of her mind. They'd been in this house for two days. Which, fine, wasn't long in the big scheme of the entire world. But they couldn't even go outside while they waited.

Waited, waited, waited. *Bah.*

She took the medicine ball that Adalyn had dropped off and threw it at the kitchen door, took perverse pleasure when it made a big bang then popped back to her.

Normally she ran for exercise, but that was out for now—though Adalyn had offered to get her a treadmill. But she was holding off until they knew how long they'd be stuck here.

Until then she was doing medicine ball squats and throws.

Squat down, pop up, throw the ball at the door. Boom. She did it again.

"What the—"

She caught the ball and turned to find a shirtless Colin with a pistol in his hand staring at her. At least the weapon was at his side.

"What are you doing?"

"Seems pretty obvious to me." Her tone was a little rude, but she was feeling rude. And cranky, and all the things in between. She hated everything at the moment, including herself. Her stupid, sabotaging asshole self.

"I thought someone was breaking in," he muttered.

Ignoring him, she threw the ball again, caught it.

"Mari."

She turned to find he'd set his weapon down so she threw the ball at him. He caught it with a surprised expression.

"Come on. Do it with me. You need to let off some steam too."

"I'm not doing whatever it is you're doing," he said as he tossed the ball at her.

Feeling smug, she squatted, popped up and threw it. "It's cool, I know it's a lot of work for someone your age."

"I'm only a few years older than you," he grumbled as he did the squat. "And for the record, I feel ridiculous," he added as he threw the ball back at her.

"Who cares? No one's here to see us." The others were all gone for now, but she knew one or two of them would be back in time for dinner. Or if they had news. But at this point, she figured they were never getting out of here. And it wasn't like she and Colin were having sex. "Have you talked to your partners?" she asked.

"Yeah." He grunted slightly at her harder throw. "Everything's good. Might have some new clients."

"Thank your partners again for me. I've heard from two clients that they were total pros."

He nodded, and thankfully they didn't talk after that, but simply let out their aggression and energy on the ball—because again, they weren't going to be having sex.

Not when he was barely talking to her. And she hated how much she cared. See? This was why you had to keep your heart out of things. Because after sex everything got weird and stupid.

They both paused at the sound of the door opening. Sweaty and exhausted and so grateful for the interruption—though she'd never admit it because she hadn't wanted to be the one who quit first—she turned to find Berlin and Chance stepping inside.

Berlin blinked at the two of them. "I'm scared to ask what you've been doing."

"Exercise."

"Fun." Berlin's tone was dry.

"You're here so please tell me you have good news." She wasn't sure how long they'd been squatting and throwing that damn ball at each other but her thighs were shaking so bad she was ready to fall over. She refused to show how tired she was though. Instead of collapsing on her face, she strode to the fridge and grabbed two bottles of water and tossed one to Colin.

"Oh yeah. I've had a busy two days." Berlin sat at the island top and set her laptop on it as Chance disappeared into the bedrooms.

Mari had learned by now that anytime anyone stopped by, they checked out the house to make sure everything was secure. It might be overkill but she was okay with it. Having armed gunman chase after her and Colin had really changed her perspective on things.

"From what I've found and what the DEA has confirmed—"

"They talked to you?"

Berlin snorted. "Ah, not exactly. Let's just say some of the information I've got came from Camila, a friend of one of my bosses and my awesome skills."

Mari grinned as she leaned against the countertop across from Berlin. Colin was right next to her, somehow smelling way too good for a man who'd just spent a long time working out with her. How was that possible? Unfair, that was what it was.

"From what the DEA has found, Ackerman was definitely working for the Suarez cartel. He's been moving stuff for them for about the last year. According to his wife—who the DEA interviewed, and Camila has confirmed that she saw the interview video—he started acting off about a year ago. He said he was working with some new clients, and while she was pretty sure that what he was doing was illegal, he didn't seem scared. Just guilty almost. She even thought he might be having an affair. But then a month ago, she says he was actually scared. He told her that he was in over his head and that if he ever called and told her to run, she had to take their daughter and leave. Find friends or relatives to stay with and not even tell him where they were. He was worried he might be tortured and didn't want to give away their location."

"That's intense," Colin murmured.

Berlin nodded. "Agreed. She said she talked to a divorce attorney then because he scared her so much. Then he told her that he had a plan to keep them all alive, safe. That he was getting leverage."

"I can see where this is going," Mari murmured.

"Yep." Berlin's tone was dry. "He took something. She doesn't know exactly what, but said he was planning to steal or copy records. Something that would give their family a way out. That's all she claims to know. The DEA has torn apart their house but hasn't found anything yet."

Chance strode back into the room then, but was quiet as he slid onto the island seat next to his fiancée.

"I know this is a long shot, but did she know anything about me?" Mari asked. "Maybe the reason he wanted people to kill me?"

"Nope. And she wasn't even sure who he worked for. He told her he was taking something from his boss. If I had to guess, it's going to be accounting records or photos of something really bad. Maybe both."

"What about the paid killers?" Colin asked, his voice flinty.

"They've already been processed and are officially in the system. They're not getting bail, not that they're asking for it. They've both confessed but have asked for specific accommodations and for a lesser sentence if they give up intel."

"On the cartel?" Mari asked.

"That I don't know. I just know they confessed to being hired by Ackerman to kill you. According to them, you knew something or overheard something."

"Except that I didn't."

Berlin shrugged. "That's what they've said. Do you remember exactly what you overheard him say?"

"Something about not liking the new direction someone was going. I didn't recognize the voice of the man he was talking to though. The man had a hint of an accent but I couldn't even tell you where from."

"According to the DEA, the Suarez cartel has started moving weapons along with drugs. And potentially people, which wouldn't surprise me at all because those organizations are all pieces of shit. If he thought you overheard him and that you were jeopardizing his chance to get leverage or whatever... I don't know. Maybe he wanted to tie up any loose threads. His wife made it sound like he was getting ready to run with her and their daughter once he had what he needed."

"What about the hired guns? Did they say anything else about Mari?" Colin asked, his tone hard.

"No. She was just a job to them. And two of the people who work at the original branch of Redemption Harbor have some...experience with hired killers."

"Hit men?" Mari asked.

"Yes. They've reached out to old contacts and scoured the message boards. There are no contracts on you. On either of you," Berlin added. "And I haven't found any hint of anyone doing a search on either of your names. And no one out of the ordinary has been to either of your houses. Or your parents' houses," she added, looking between the two of them. "We've still got people watching them."

More relief slid through her veins. "Does this mean we can leave?"

Berlin paused, then looked at Chance.

"Yes," he said, glancing back at them. "We've looked at this from all angles, and with the information we have now, there is absolutely nothing that says anyone wants to kill you anymore. But you're Berlin's friend and she wants to keep you wrapped up in cotton for two more weeks."

Mari snort-laughed as she looked at her friend. "I adore you."

"And I adore you. And...I so want to hug you now, but you're kinda gross."

"You're gross," Mari muttered, but smiled.

Berlin grinned at her. "Look, I can't find any active threats against you. But I'm still worried about you. I think you could probably go home and be fine, but I don't know. I don't love it."

"What about work? Maybe I could work but stay somewhere else instead of home? At least for a few days?" She missed flying, missed being up in the air and leaving all the bullshit of the world behind. Flying truly was the best therapy. And orgasms.

"I don't hate that."

"How about you store your plane at my hangar for the next couple weeks, just to mix things up?" Colin asked.

She looked at him, nodded. "I can live with that." There was a lot more she wanted to say to him, but now wasn't the time.

It seemed as if they could go back to their real lives. Or at least cautiously return to them.

And she was pretty sure that she wasn't invited into Colin's life.

Chapter 32

Colin glanced at his phone screen, but there was nothing. He'd have heard the alert from a text or call but at this point, checking his cell was turning into a compulsion. Because he was pretty sure he'd screwed up. Or at least contributed to the problem. Both he and Mari had screwed up.

"What?" Colin blinked at Gino, who was sitting across the table with Oliver.

"I asked who are you waiting on to call?" Gino asked—likely repeated, given his expression.

He was at the hangar with Gino, Oliver, and Bradford and Tiago who'd wanted a poker night. Though Colin was certain they'd only come along to watch out for him from any potential threats.

As if he wasn't fully trained, but he liked the two men and they were friends with Mari. He cleared his throat. "No one."

"He's waiting on Mari Kim to call him," Bradford said as he tossed his cards down. "I fold."

"Why are you waiting on her to call?" Gino asked. "Why not call her?"

"Because he screwed up." This was from Ollie, who was guarding his cards like a dragon guarding its hoard.

Which meant he had a good hand. *Damn it.* Colin tossed his cards down. "I didn't do anything."

"Clearly," Tiago murmured.

Colin frowned at the other man. He'd only talked to him a few times. "What does that mean?"

The man who was far too good looking for mere mortals gave him an arch look. "Mari is smart and level-headed."

"Mostly." She was also a runner, something he'd realized. So he should have chased after her. But she was driving him crazy and he was apparently as stubborn as she was.

Tiago arched an eyebrow. "I'm playing the odds that you screwed up. You either didn't do something you should have. Or you did something you shouldn't have."

"That logic makes no sense."

"Maybe..." Tiago tossed his winning hand down with a grin.

Ollie cursed under his breath and glared at his own cards.

"I'm not having this conversation with you guys," Colin muttered. There was no conversation to have anyway. He hadn't done anything wrong. "Mari doesn't want anyone to know about us," he blurted, then winced. How pathetic did that sound? But it was the truth and it was the crux of his issues. He wanted everyone to know they were together, but she'd been so damn intent on hiding the two of them.

Bradford blinked. "You sure about that?"

"Yeah. For the record, I don't want to be talking about this shit, but yeah. When we were all at...the *place*," he said, not spelling it out for Gino and Ollie because he wasn't sure what they should and shouldn't know about at this point. They knew some of the basics, but he hadn't told them every little detail. For plausible deniability later. Just in case. "She said she didn't want everyone in her personal business."

Bradford blinked. "That's it?"

"There was more to it than that, but yeah. She just wants to be friends with benefits."

"No way Mari said that." Bradford was already shaking his head before Colin had finished.

"Not exactly that, no." He shifted in his seat, aware that everyone was watching him and not playing cards. "But she didn't seem to want a relationship."

"Didn't seem to? The woman who was running for her life after someone sabotaged her plane? She didn't have all the answers, huh?" Bradford's tone was dry.

Colin gritted his teeth, then shoved out a sigh. "I told her that I wanted to take her out on a real date after everything, and she wanted to talk about it after... Yep, now that I'm saying this shit out loud I realize what a dumbass I am. Oh. Ooooh. I am dumb." She'd been in a high stress, life and death situation, and he probably should have chilled out and met her where she was emotionally. He should have been patient. Not something he was great at.

"This at least explains the weird energy when you two were in the safe house," Bradford said. "Did you guys talk at all the last couple days?"

"Kinda. We worked out a couple times together—and no that's not a euphemism. But we didn't...actually talk much after getting back from...the place. Right about now I'm questioning how the hell I've been functioning as an adult. What the hell is wrong with me?"

"You've never been in a real relationship. Give yourself a break." Gino shrugged as he shuffled the cards.

"I've been in relationships."

"Eh." Ollie snort-laughed as Gino shook his head.

"I've dated."

"Dating and real adult relationships are different."

Sighing, he picked up the cards as Gino started dealing. He should have just told Mari how he was feeling and what he truly wanted between them, but he'd felt hurt, like she was rejecting him and he'd reacted like a bull. But Jesus, she hadn't been. She just hadn't wanted to talk about stuff in the middle of what was essentially an op. And even if she had been rejecting him, he still should have talked to her like an adult.

He'd let old shit from his childhood, old baggage, get in his head. He had a very complicated relationship with his parents in that they never talked about anything real. His parents had always had certain expectations for both him and Bear. And neither he nor his brother had done anything with their lives that their parents envisioned. He was really good at burying his feelings, shutting down when shit got too hard.

But he couldn't do that with Mari. He had to step up and be the man she needed. And hell, the man he needed. If he wanted something real with her, he had to start unpacking all his old bullshit.

He scrubbed a hand over his face, then picked up his phone, not bothering to even check his cards. "I'm going to step outside, I'll be back."

Instead of texting, he called Mari—and to his disappointment was sent to voicemail after two rings. But this wasn't over, he would make things right—he had to.

CHAPTER 33

It's my first life; I'm still figuring things out.

Mari stopped inside her parents' kitchen to find her grandmother making tea. "Hey, I didn't realize you were home today. I thought you had your art group." It was Saturday and that meant "art club," which meant going to various museums or to see private collections—and her group also offered scholarships to high school students. Her grandmother had more of a social life than Mari, something she chose not to dwell on.

She was also part of some sort of "sneaker club" that Mari didn't totally understand, as well as a book club and of course she was part of an Asian krewe for Mardi Gras which kept her busy year-round. Seriously, the woman was incredible. But she always found time to go flying with Mari and had been her biggest supporter all those years ago when she'd decided to go for her dreams.

"That's not until this afternoon. Tea?"

Mari nodded and pulled out the teacups her halmeoni preferred. "I like your outfit. It's going to slay at your meeting."

Her grandmother sniffed as if to say *of course*. In wide-legged vintage floral pants and a chic button-down blouse, she could blend in anywhere.

But add in the metallic purple sneakers and matching metallic belt bag, she stood out in all the best ways. She'd pulled her dark hair back into a twist, and even though she complained about the length, always threatening to cut it, Mari knew she never would. Her grandfather had liked it too much so she kept it long.

"Other than Magnolia, who are your friends outside?" she asked softly.

Mari glanced over her shoulder through the glass doors to the pool beyond. After being officially freed yesterday from the safe house, she'd come to her parents' house, mostly because she'd known they'd gone on a last-minute out of town trip.

Despite her issues with her mother, she still felt safe here. This place was basically a fortress and she'd wanted the familiarity of her childhood home.

"Ah, just some work friends." Which wasn't exactly right, but it was easier to say that than explain how she knew everyone.

Her friends, knowing how much she'd needed them, had come over this morning for a "pool party" which made her feel like she was in high school again. But she loved that they were all getting to relax together. It made her feel normal after the insanity of the last few days. So Magnolia, Berlin, Adalyn, Fleur, and even Camila were here for mimosas and sun. Two of her pilot friends were supposed to come by in an hour as well. She could have taken over one of the jobs she'd handed off but had decided to give herself one more day.

Maybe two if she took off tomorrow as well. She needed to get her head on straight anyway.

"So what is going on, my sweet girl?"

"Nothing much."

"Don't lie to me."

Mari cleared her throat, wondering how her halmeoni always saw through her. "Just...dealing with some stuff. How did you know Harabeoji was the one for you?"

If she was surprised by the question, her grandmother didn't show it. Instead she sat at the table that looked out onto the backyard and patio beyond where Mari's friends were all relaxing and enjoying the sunny day. Even Berlin, who had been cannonballing earlier, was now lying out with everyone. They all looked so peaceful. Mari sat next to her grandmother and took a sip of the lemon green tea.

"He listened and he made me laugh…and he was the bravest person I ever knew."

Mari knew the story of how her grandfather had made the decision to come to America, how he'd been brave enough to ask her grandmother to go with him even though her parents disapproved. How they'd still sent money back for years, how they'd struggled so their daughter could have a better education than they'd had. Sometimes if she really thought about all the things her halmeoni had done in her lifetime it was staggering.

"But the way he truly listened is why I fell for him. You remind me a lot of him."

She blinked. "I do?"

Her grandmother nodded. "You were always the outlaw in this family and so was he."

"Outlaw?"

"I'm certain it is the right word."

Mari grinned. "I think I'll get that on a T-shirt." *Outlaw, hell yeah.*

"You've never lived your life for anyone else's approval. Even when you were small. It frustrates your mother, but she respects you for it."

"Yeah, I don't know about that."

Her grandmother simply sighed. "Who is this man making you ask questions about my past?"

"No one, just sort of abstract questioning."

Her halmeoni just gave her a look that said she knew she was lying. Then she patted Mari's hand gently as she stood. "Well, I'm sure you'll figure things out. And hopefully that nice Lockhart boy figures out how to win your heart."

She blinked as her grandmother left the room, but knew she shouldn't be surprised. Sometimes Mari swore she was psychic.

"Hey, what's taking so long?" Magnolia stepped into the kitchen, her baby bump more pronounced now than it had been just days ago. Especially since she was wearing a two-piece bathing suit and wrap.

"Nothing."

"Oh, I want some tea. Did your grandma leave?"

"She's got one of her clubs soon."

"I'm jealous of her energy," Magnolia said as she poured a cup for herself.

"Same."

"Please, you have just as much. And I'm so impressed that you're so chill after the last few days. I'd be freaking out."

"Uh, no, you wouldn't." And her best friend had handled her own bullshit after the insanity of earlier this year.

"Fine, you're right, but you've dealt with a lot for anyone. So what's going on with you and Colin? I've given you enough time to tell me and now I'm pulling the pregnancy card and best friend card at the same time. I'm hormonal and your bestie and I want to know. Right now."

Laughing, she resumed her seat at the table with Magnolia, who'd laid her hand on her stomach and was cupping it protectively. "I can't ignore those cards. And I don't know what's going on. I screwed up. That much I know. I keep trying to get a handle on my feelings for him, to keep a level head and—"

"Oh my god, Mari!"

"What?"

"When you're in love with someone you can't always get a handle on your feelings. Emotions like love can't be boxed up or controlled. And I know and appreciate how much you like to control situations but you *can't* do that with love."

Mari sputtered. "I don't love..." Oh. Oh god. *Oh. My. God.* She did love him. "I love him?"

"Uh yeah. I thought you already knew that."

"What the hell is wrong with me! I can't be in love with my brother's best friend."

"Why not? He's great."

"He's kinda bossy. And fine, gorgeous. And oh no. Nooooo." Mari covered her face with her hands. "This makes things so much worse. I can't see him right now. I need to keep some distance while I get a handle... Oh, I hear myself now. I'm insane."

Magnolia simply nodded and lifted her teacup to her mouth. "Your words, not mine."

Mari looked down into her tea as she realized that yep, she was in love with Colin. Which really did make things worse. So. Much. Worse. Because he'd been talking about going on a date.

Not anything else more serious. Oh, she did not like this feeling at all. No wonder she'd stuck to loving her planes all her adult life. Planes were better than anything else.

Now she had to deal with all these dumbass emotions that wanted to take over everything. Well, not today. She set her tea down and headed for the fridge and grabbed the already open bottle of champagne. Tea wasn't going to cut it.

So she was going to do what any rational adult did when faced with a problem. Drink alcohol.

CHAPTER 34

I don't catch feelings, I catch flights.

It was seven in the morning, so not terribly early. Not for pilots anyway. But as Mari drove, she was questioning her decision to just show up at Colin's house like this.

She hadn't been able to sleep all night after talking to Magnolia. Was she really in love with Colin? Dumb question, she was. Annoyingly so.

Which explained why she was pulling down his street before breakfast like a total stalker. Sighing, she pulled up to the curb and called him. Because yeah, showing up like this was all about her manic need right now and she had to calm the heck down. This was not how someone started a relationship. Or she assumed it wasn't.

His phone rang and rang, finally going to voicemail so she hung up. She wasn't sure what to say if he'd answered, much less to his voicemail. Now she was really glad she hadn't just shown up because she would have been drowning in embarrassment later.

Sighing to herself, she'd slid her Jeep into drive when she spotted a tall redhead with messy bed head walking out the front door of his place. She blinked, her stomach twisting in knots.

The sight was like a slap of cold water to the face. The woman was wearing a short, sparkly red dress someone would wear to a club and carrying a little matching clutch purse. She slid sunglasses on as she made her way to the sleek Mercedes parked on the curb in front of the neighbor's house.

Mari stared as the woman drove off, as if she could somehow figure out why some woman was leaving his place so early. But come on, she knew why.

And it absolutely gutted her.

She couldn't even be mad at him about it (lies, she was pissed). They weren't anything. They'd slept together, that was it.

There had been no words of commitment. *Nothing*.

This was on her and she kind of hated herself in that moment.

Him too if she was being brutally honest. It certainly didn't take him any time to move on from her.

Angrily, she swiped away her tears and pulled away from the curb to head home. Love was bullshit.

CHAPTER 35

Two days later

"Thanks for the last-minute flight." Gary tossed his small duffel in the back before sliding into his seat, putting on his headset, and buckling up.

"Of course. Thank you for being so patient this last week. I hope you're not going to throw me over for another pilot," Mari said jokingly.

He snorted. "Never."

"I'm impressed you got a replacement so fast." The plane she was flying today was a basic mirror of his other one, with the exception of the leather interior color. This one was more of a buttercream as opposed to caramel.

"Money talks."

"Apparently. Any news on the plane?"

He sighed, shrugged as she finished up the preflight. Once she was done and rolling toward the taxiway, he said, "So did you hear anything more from law enforcement?"

"Nope. Well other than having to make an official report with NTSB. What about you? Are they answering questions for your insurance? Hopefully they're not giving you too much grief."

"Everything's fine on my end. We'll get it all sorted." He didn't seem concerned, which made sense considering how much money she suspected he made.

At least that was one thing she didn't have to worry about. And even though she knew the sabotage wasn't her fault, she'd still felt bad about the whole thing.

Once she got departure clearance from the tower, they were off, the takeoff perfect and a good omen for the day. As they hit the three thousand feet AGL mark she could feel the last two days of internal stress fall away in the slipstream.

Mostly.

She was still a mess inside, but no one was trying to kill her and she was back to work, doing the thing she loved most. She'd get to the mental place she needed eventually. If only Colin would stop calling her. After seeing that woman leave his house, she'd decided to ignore his calls.

To be fair he'd only called twice, yesterday and the day before. But she didn't even want to see his name on her caller ID. She was thinking about him the majority of the time, and seeing his name just slid the knife deeper. Seriously, love was a crock of shit. Who wanted to deal with all these emotions? Ugh. Not her.

"Did you see about Jeremy Ackerman?" Gary's voice came over the comm line, startling her.

"Yeah. That was a shock to see his name on the news." Luckily she hadn't been mentioned at all. At least not yet, and she hoped it stayed that way. His murder had made even the New Orleans local news, mainly because he lived here and was rich, she was pretty sure. But they'd also mentioned potential ties to organized crime and how he'd been under investigation by the DEA when he'd been killed.

"You think you know someone," he muttered, looking out the window.

"Right?" She wasn't up for conversation today and thankfully Gary ended up pulling out his tablet and answering emails. Which was how they did things most days.

So she settled into doing her job, flying, monitoring the sky around them and trying not to obsess about a certain tall, ridiculously handsome pilot who'd stolen her heart.

And she nailed two of those things.

***

"This is just plain weird," Berlin muttered.

Bradford was pretty sure she was talking more to herself than him. In fact, he was pretty sure she wasn't even aware he was in her office. She had been at one point, but she tended to tune all of them out for the most part.

After the mess with Mari and Colin, they were back to normal, looking at a handful of job requests that had come in and deciding which ones to work on first. The work they did was mostly from word of mouth, but as he glanced over her shoulder he realized she was looking at something to do with Mari. The back of his neck prickled in alarm. "What is?"

"Oh shit. Didn't realize you were there. What are you doing?" she asked without looking up.

"You stole all the little cakes so I came to grab a few."

"They're called petit fours, and they're all mine."

"Not anymore," he said around a mouthful, enjoying the glare she shot over her shoulder. "So what's weird? That doesn't look like a new case." He chin-nodded at the split screen. There was an image of Five C's Aviation on it.

"It's not. And I don't know if this is anything or not, but the way

Ackerman was killed just felt too neat to me."

"Torture feels neat?"

"Not that. I still can't figure out why he would want to kill Mari. Send actual *trained* killers after her. Hired guns. It's too weird and I don't like not knowing the why of things."

"I hear ya." He popped another tiny cake in his mouth, enjoyed the explosion of strawberry and cream.

"If you eat another one, I'm not responsible for what I might do."

"These were a gift to the *office*, not you specifically."

She just sniffed. "Fine. Hand me one, will you?"

He grabbed the platter—yes, platter—that she'd stolen from the break room along with a chair and sat next to her. Holding it out, he tried to follow what she was doing, but more often than not it was just gibberish on screen.

This time, however, it was different. "Is that the woman from Five C's?" The rude, red-headed receptionist.

"Yep. It was just a hunch but I started digging into her. Her behavior was so over-the-top rude, yet she holds on to her job. She's pretty enough, but that kind of shit doesn't usually fly anywhere. Pun intended." She grabbed two petit fours, shoved them in her mouth before she continued tapping away on her keyboard.

"She's related to the owner. At least that's what Blanca said. Maybe she's actually screwing the owner."

"Nope. I don't think so… There." Berlin frowned at the screen, which was showing a grainy birth certificate now. "Huh. That's the same last name as—"

"Oh. Shit." Bradford stared at the screen, trying to make sense of it. "So Gary Sewall is this Heidi's father?"

"It would appear so. And he's the owner of Five C's Aviation. It's buried deep but I finally found a small connection between…"

Bradford tuned out the tech talk as she went on, catching about a third of it this time. Finally he said, "So he owns the company that Ackerman uses—used—but doesn't actually use it himself?"

"No. It's like he's compartmentalized different parts of his life. And he's done such an incredible job, I wouldn't have found this if not for the link to his daughter. And I had to look *really* hard. This makes no sense. If he owns the company, why not use it? Why use small corporate pilots for his daily life?"

"It's a cover," Bradford said, because it was the only thing that made sense. "Has to be. The guy is a political consultant and flies all over the southeast, usually with Mari. If I had to guess, it's like you said, he's compartmentalizing parts of his life so they don't cross over with each other. It's something that people involved in organized crime do. Cartels or… Oh, Jesus." He watched as Berlin continued to work, his stomach twisting. "Mari is flying with him right now."

Berlin stilled for a moment, cursed under her breath, but kept working as she muttered, "Hold on."

But he wasn't holding for anything. He already had his phone out and had pulled up Colin's name. Because there was no way they could get to Mari in time with her being in the air. Adalyn was their only pilot—so far—and she'd headed to north Florida this morning.

As he hit send on his text, Berlin sat back and looked at the screen.

He wondered when the last time she'd slept was. "Am I seeing this right?"

"There is no Suarez cartel. Not really. It's a cover he created. He's a criminal mastermind." She sounded in awe, or maybe horror, of it. "I've still got more layers to peel back, more bank accounts to hack, but…" She shook her head. "Gary Sewall is essentially, the Suarez cartel." Her expression worried, she turned to look at him. "You're sure Mari is with him?"

"Yeah, she texted me this morning. Said it was back to work as usual for her. We talked about other stuff... Not important. I've already texted Colin, he's on his way to her now."

Bradford just hoped Colin could make it to Mari in time. There shouldn't be any reason for Gary to kill her, not that she'd let on about. But someone had tried to kill her more than once and now Ackerman was dead and tortured, likely not long after he'd taken that flight with Mari.

Something had happened on that flight, Bradford was sure of it.

CHAPTER 36

If you like high class escorts, squawk 7500.

Colin couldn't contain the fear punching through him as he flew north, desperate to get to Mari.

"We're going to get there in time." Gino was sitting next to him, had jumped into the plane despite Colin's protests that he had things handled.

Not that he'd wasted much time, not when Bradford had told him Mari was likely with the man who'd wanted her dead. Gary Sewall, one of her longtime clients, a man she considered a friend. It didn't make sense to Colin, but it didn't have to make sense.

He just had to get to her before anything happened.

He'd called in a favor to a friend at ATC who'd confirmed when Mari had left and what her flight plan was. So he simply had to beat her, to get there faster and be there when she landed. If Sewall had anything planned, Colin doubted he'd do it with witnesses around.

Though at this point, he didn't know shit about the guy except that he'd likely sent hired guns after them and was apparently the mastermind behind a cartel. So maybe he didn't care about witnesses.

"I know," he said to Gino, even though he wasn't sure at all.

"I'm impressed you stole Frank's plane."

"I borrowed it." Big difference. His client's plane—which Frank took out eight times a year—had just been sitting there. And the Mooney would get him there faster than his own Cessna.

Gino simply grunted.

Colin didn't care. He'd have stolen an F-22 if he'd had access to one. Anything for Mari. He loved her, simple as that. He'd set the world on fire for her and he should have just shown up at her place, demanded she listen to him.

He'd been too worried about all the wrong things, like not pushing her too fast. Apparently he should have pushed her harder, locked her down, made it crystal clear how important she was to him.

He refused to accept that it might be too late now. He was going to find her and make sure she was safe.

"That's the Cirrus," he said into his headset as he and Gino flew a thousand feet above the plane Mari was piloting. He wished he could reach out to her, check in with her. Hell, if he was wishing, he wished she was at his place in bed with him right now instead of up here.

But reaching out over the radio to her was far too dangerous. He couldn't risk accidentally tipping off Sewall by saying the wrong thing. She was currently piloting for the guy so she was safe.

She was alive. And he was going to make sure she stayed that way.

Chapter 37

Life is short and complicated, just like me.

"Am I picking you up this afternoon or are you planning to stay longer?" Mari asked as she parked the plane in front of the fueling pumps. They hadn't talked specifics yet, which was pretty common for Gary. She really didn't envy him his job, having to work with politicians all the time, to be at the whim of their schedules.

Though clearly he must like it, or the very expensive things it afforded him—like the replacement plane he'd gotten as a loan until his was fixed. She was just glad his insurance was covering everything.

He'd stepped out of the plane, was stretching as she headed to the pump. "This afternoon is the plan, but if anything changes I'll let you know before you leave."

"Perfect." She was glad she didn't have to use a stepstool to fuel this particular plane. The fuel access points were on the leading edge of each wing, like most single-engine planes. But with this one, the wings were lower, something her short girl self, appreciated. With Cessnas and Pipers, she could technically reach up and touch the access points, but forget about actually unscrewing the caps and pumping fuel. All part of her short girl life.

As she connected the grounding cable in preparation to pump, she saw Gary reaching in and tugging her backpack out of the seat. She frowned at him, wondering what he was doing.

But then he smiled at her. "Just grabbing my water bottle," he said as he pulled it out from underneath.

She grinned at him and ducked back out to start the refueling process. Once she was done, she parked the plane outside instead of in the hangar, then headed for the little diner to grab her burritos to go.

Everything was pretty much back to normal. "Yay," she muttered to herself as she grabbed her cell phone from her bag. When she saw missed calls from Berlin, Bradford and Colin, she frowned.

She called Berlin back first since she'd called *eight* times. "Hey—"

"Are you safe?" Berlin demanded.

She straightened at her friend's urgent tone. "Ah, yeah. What's going on?"

"Your client Gary Sewall is behind everything."

Ice slid through her even as she stepped out into the sunshine, burrito bag in hand. But her mind butted up against her friend's words. "No way."

"I'm not wrong about this. I have a ton of evidence, all of which I'll let you look at, but get the hell back home."

She turned back toward the diner, intending to sit down—or let her legs collapse on one of the booths. But she found herself face-to-face with her long-time client, Gary Sewall. Somehow, she found her voice, faked a smile. "Hey, Gary..."

That was when she saw the pistol in his hand. He held it low by his waist, his windbreaker hiding most of it. Not that anyone was outside. Nope, the few customers were inside eating and there was no one landing or taking off.

Berlin had gone silent on the other end of the line, but it didn't matter because he plucked Mari's phone out of her hand, pressed the end button, then tucked it into his pocket.

"If you make a sound, I'll shoot you where you stand and then I'll kill everyone in the diner." The look in his eyes was terrifying. Flat. Calm. The eyes of a killer.

Mari felt as if she was staring at a stranger, not the man she'd spent years flying, but she was smart enough to nod. Because she didn't think he was lying. There was a coldness in his eyes she'd never seen before, as if he'd just taken off a mask and shown her the real man beneath.

Not the perpetually exhausted middle-aged man who made dad jokes and recommended her services to people he knew on the regular. Instead, he seemed to be standing a little straighter and his hand wasn't wavering at all. It was clear this man had killed before.

And he would absolutely shoot her if she made a wrong move.

As fear trickled down her spine, she started to put her hands up on instinct, but he hissed.

"No. Act natural and walk to the hangar. I don't want to hurt you, but I will."

Feeling numb, she did as he said and turned around, strode toward the hangar, simultaneously hoping someone was there, while also hoping it was empty. She didn't want anyone else to get caught in the crossfire, but she still hoped someone could help, call the cops, something. In that moment, she hated what a coward she'd been with Colin. She was likely going to die today and she wouldn't get to tell him how she felt.

"I hate that it's come to this." His voice was low, casual, calm as they made their way across the tarmac.

They walked past his plane and a couple others before the hangar opening came into view, the rolling door up.

She thought of Ackerman dying in a place like this. Her insides turned liquid. Would he torture her too? Or order someone else to do it? Oh god, she was going to puke.

"I didn't feel bad about Ackerman, but I do feel bad about you. You will have to die, of course, but I won't make you suffer."

"Why?" Mari managed to rasp out.

"I mirrored your phone when you unlocked it this morning in the plane, so I heard your conversation with your little friend. Whoever she is, I assume it's who helped you get back to New Orleans and avoid the couple I sent after you. And why? Money, my dear. And power, more than that. But it's the things that money can buy, if I'm being specific."

"Fancy planes?" She couldn't keep the derision out of her voice. This piece of shit had hunted her and Colin, and now he was going to kill her if she didn't figure out a way to escape in the next few minutes.

"I don't care about that. Though it is nice to be able to travel without having to interact with others. But that's not why I do this. I would explain it to you if I felt you could fully understand, but not many people do. I've created the world I want to live in, and I won't let anyone else get in my way."

"Like your friend Ackerman?"

Now he actually laughed. "That moron wasn't my friend. To the world I let it appear as if he was an associate because it helped with the persona I've created. The smart political consultant who indulges his wife and has two vacation homes he lets friends use." He sounded as if he was reading a sound bite. "In reality, Ackerman was just another tool. Albeit an annoying one, but the man had a lot of contacts and an in with a shipping company I've been trying to get into bed with for years."

"So... he didn't want to kill me?" She was pretty sure no, but wanted all the details. It was clear Gary planned to kill her and she figured she deserved that.

"No, he didn't. And for the record, those morons weren't supposed to kill you."

"The two shooters... I remember... I recognize the man from the hangar in New Orleans. I've seen him around before." When she'd seen that man standing by the Land Rover at the bed and breakfast, she knew she'd recognized him from somewhere.

Gary simply nodded. "I needed to know what Ackerman told you on that flight. My people were simply supposed to figure out what he took from me and gave to you. The plane was supposed to go down and they were supposed to take your bag. They disabled the parachute system, and set the EMP—which they would have retrieved later. It was all so neat and tidy. Or it should have been." He sighed as if annoyed about the weather.

"He didn't tell me anything. Or give me anything." She didn't touch on the part where the plane was supposed to go down. He either had a lot of faith in her flying skills or he just hadn't cared if she had died. She was guessing it was the latter, considering the pistol he was holding like a pro and the fact that he'd had his people disable the parachute system.

"That's exactly what he told my men. But he was lying. Unfortunately he had a heart attack and died before we could finish with him. That's far enough."

They were halfway into the hangar now, near a plane that looked... Wait a minute. She realized they were standing next to the same Mooney she'd seen at Colin's hangar. It was the same call sign.

Her heart jumped. Colin couldn't be here, could he? No, that was ridiculous. She was just desperately hoping someone would save her.

She turned to face Gary, but kept her movements measured. She didn't want him to accidentally shoot her.

Though with the casual grip he had on his weapon, she didn't think he'd make a mistake.

"Drop your backpack on the ground and kick it over to me."

"My backpack?"

"Jesus, Mari, don't repeat everything I'm saying. Just do it." He quickly glanced behind him to make sure no one was coming.

She wondered what the plan was. There weren't any cameras inside the hangar, but there were a couple outside of it. And at least one in the parking lot. She didn't think he'd kill her here, so he'd want to move her somewhere else. Maybe that would give her a small opening.

But she had to do what he said right now. With trembling hands, she dropped her bag of burritos, then she slid her backpack off and kicked it over to him. Out of the corner of her eye, she saw movement behind a vintage red and white Piper Cub.

She couldn't risk looking in that direction in case someone was back there.

Gary crouched down and began rummaging through her backpack, dumping out her protein bars, extra clothes, water. Then he unzipped the zipper in the back interior and pulled out a small flash drive.

"That's not mine."

The relief that flashed across his face sent fear snaking down her spine. Whatever he was looking for, he'd clearly found it. Ackerman must have put it in her backpack the day she flew him.

A loud crash from across the hangar had them both turning.

Gary slightly lowered his weapon as he looked toward where the sound had come from.

And then a blur of muscle sprinted out from behind the Piper.

CHAPTER 38

Woke up today, chose violence.

Colin had never had a problem being patient—until today.

But he forced himself to remain hidden as Gary Sewall, a walking dead man, ordered Mari deeper into the hangar.

Gary's gun hand never wavered as they walked. That was definitely going to be a problem. If Colin had had a weapon on him when Bradford had called, this would be a different ball game, but he never brought it with him to work. And there had been no time to go home first.

Since Sewall was so steady even as he dug through Mari's backpack, Colin shot off a quick text to Gino, who was hiding on the other side of the hangar behind a sport plane.

A few moments later, a small rack of paint cans upended, bouncing onto the concrete with a loud crash, one after the other.

Colin moved the instant Sewall turned around, sprinting right at him.

At the last moment, Sewall heard or sensed him, Colin wasn't sure. Didn't matter.

It was as if everything happened in slow motion as Sewall raised his pistol.

But there was no stopping now.

He barreled into Sewall like a linebacker. The gun went off, the explosion echoing through the hangar. He heard it clatter to the ground, but couldn't reach it.

Instead, he slammed Sewall to the concrete, aware of nothing but the raw need to incapacitate him. End this threat to Mari.

Pain splintered through his left side as Sewall slammed a fist into his ribs. He wasn't sure why the strike was so damn painful until he saw the blood on the concrete. Not a fist.

Fury rushed through him as he landed a punch to Sewall's jaw, his head ricocheting onto the concrete below. Then another one, and another one.

Sewall punched his kidney, but Colin managed to roll him onto his front, pin him facedown. As he went to yank Sewall's hands behind his back, the bastard grasped the fallen pistol. But before he could fully grab it, Mari screamed and slammed her sneaker down onto his hand.

Gino was right behind her, scooping up the pistol.

She stomped on Sewall's hand again with another savage shout, definitely breaking the man's bones. Sewall cried out in agony, bucking under him.

Adrenaline rode Colin hard as he finally wrenched Sewall's hands behind his back.

"Here." Gino handed him a bungee cord he'd gotten from who knew where, but it worked for securing Sewall's wrists. "I've already called the cops," his friend added.

"Good." Spots danced before Colin's eyes as he fell back on his ass, just grateful that Sewall was bound.

He thought Gino murmured, "Oh shit," but then Mari was in front of him, her expression concerned. He cried out when she pressed on the wound in his side.

"He's losing blood too fast. We've got to get him to the nearest hospital and I'm not waiting for an ambulance!"

Those were the last words he heard before blackness took over.

CHAPTER 39

Colin opened his eyes to a consistent beeping sound, blinked slowly and took in his surroundings. It was a minute before he realized he was in a hospital. The blinds over the window were cracked open and he could see it was dark out...and there was a lump on the little bench next to his bed. He cleared his throat, looking around for water, when the lump moved.

Mari sat up, shoving a blanket off her, her eyes a little panicked. "Hey, you're awake. I'll get the doctor." He shook his head and tried to talk but she shushed him. "Hold on, here's some water."

It definitely took longer than he liked, but he sipped slowly through the straw until he felt he could talk normally. "Hey, you're okay? Where's Sewall?"

"In custody, and I'm fine. You're the one in the hospital bed." Her voice cracked on the last word as she took his hand in hers. "Also, I lied and said I was your fiancée if anyone asks," she whispered, glancing at the closed door. "Gino backed me up."

His side burned like hell. "What happened? I remember the hangar, but what happened to me?"

"That asshole stabbed you," she gritted out, fire in her dark eyes. "He hit your spleen so they had to do an emergency splenectomy, but you're going to be okay."

From her tone he couldn't tell if she was saying the words for herself or him. He tightened his grip on her hand, just wanting to touch her. When he'd seen that asshole holding a gun on her, he'd lost a decade of his life. "I'm just glad you're okay."

She held up his hand to her mouth, kissed the top of it gently as her eyes filled with tears.

"Don't cry," he rasped out. He could take the pain of a knife wound, but not her tears.

"I'm not." She kissed his hand again, but looked up when the door opened.

Gino was there, looking as exhausted as Mari, but his eyes lit up when he saw Colin. And to Colin's disappointment, Mari stood.

"I'm going to get your doctor and let the others know you're awake."

Colin wanted to tell her to stop but Gino slid into her seat, his expression worried. "Jesus, man, we thought we'd lost you."

"What did the doctor say?"

"That if you came through the surgery, you'd make it." Gino looked away for a moment, his jaw tight. "I wish I'd just killed that son of a bitch in the hangar." He seemed to shake himself, then looked back at Colin. "Your girl was something else though. She said the hospital was too far and she wasn't waiting for the ambulance, so we loaded you up into that bastard's plane and an ambulance met you and her at an airport only two miles from the hospital. It saved your life."

He didn't remember any of it. "Mari's not in trouble?"

"Hell no. She had to answer questions—so did I. But the DEA ended up taking over everything...and you know what, it doesn't matter," he said when the door opened and Mari and a woman who was clearly his doctor strode in, wearing a smile on her face.

Gino moved so Mari could sit, and Colin listened while his surgeon told him about the damage he'd sustained, how lucky he ultimately was (not the word he would have used), that he'd be in the hospital for another six days at least, and his recovery time was going to be six to eight weeks. She said a lot of other stuff, most of which he promptly forgot as he held on to Mari's hand.

Nothing else mattered at this point. The threat to Mari was over, she was finally safe, and it sounded like he'd live to see another day. So he closed his eyes and laid his head back against the pillow. Everything else could wait until after he got some more sleep.

***

One week later

"You are quite literally the worst patient in the world." Mari's tone was tempered with patience, but just barely.

"I'm sorry," he muttered. The recovery was way worse than anything they showed on TV or in movies.

She blinked at him as she helped him sit up. "What was that? Did you actually say 'I'm sorry'?"

"Come on, you can't mess with the injured man," he muttered as he slowly got out of bed. He'd been discharged the day before and was now thankfully back in New Orleans in his own home. He hadn't taken a pain pill yet today and was debating taking one at all. He hated feeling groggy, even if it did ease the hellish throbbing in his side.

"I know. And you're not the worst patient. You're incredible and…I love you." She blurted the last part out, staring up at him in terror as if she'd admitted to acts of terrorism.

Relief hit him hard and fast, and he would have laughed at the look of horror on her face if he didn't think the pain would make him black out. "Thank god, I love you too." He'd wanted to tell her the moment he'd been lucid enough, but had been worried she'd feel guilty enough to say it back without meaning it.

"Really?" She sounded so unsure.

"Not a lot of people I'd get stabbed for," he murmured, reaching out to cup her cheek.

"Liar. You'd have done that for anyone because you're an incredible human."

"You're really good for my ego." His gaze fell to her mouth, but he reined in the impulse to kiss her. Instead, he settled his hands on her hips. "And yes, I love you. Been in love with you for a while, Mari."

"Me too," she whispered even though it was just the two of them in his place.

His parents were currently out of the country but would be back next week to see him. And Mari hadn't told her brother he was home yet, which he appreciated. He wanted to see his friends, but in a few days once he was hopefully no longer in agony.

"I know I thanked you already, but what you did was incredible."

"You're the incredible one." She'd been solid even when that monster had been holding a gun on her. A man she'd worked with for years, someone she'd considered a friend. He was in a tiny cell now, and would die in one just like it.

"Pretty sure we could stand here complimenting each other all day," she murmured, gently settling her hands on his chest but not getting any closer to him. "Let's get you something to eat and then relax."

He hated that she was having to help him out and take care of him, but was simultaneously grateful. "I really want to kiss you now." Even if there was no way he could bend down, not with the damage to his muscles.

In response, she stood on the side of the bed and leaned down to kiss him. He laughed lightly, winced at the pain, then leaned into her mouth.

He loved the taste of her, how absolutely fierce she was in everything she did. If it wasn't for her quick thinking, he wasn't sure he'd be here at all. "Soon," he managed to rasp out, "we're doing more than this."

She grinned at him. "Is that really where your head is right now?"

"Always with you." Always and forever.

She looked down at him with a hint of amusement, but he wasn't joking. It was always going to be her.

CHAPTER 40

"Whoa." Mari stared at Camila for a long moment before looking back at Colin. The detective had stopped by to check on the two of them as well as update them, and the news wasn't what Mari had been expecting. She sat at the island top in his kitchen and he moved up next to her instead of sitting down. "I've been mentally prepping myself for testifying against him."

Colin simply nodded, but his eyes looked more murderous than anything. She guessed he'd just been fantasizing about doing worse to Gary Sewall. Mainly because he'd told her more than once he wished he'd just killed the guy.

Who Mari was now trying to think of as just Sewall instead of Gary, her longtime client. "He's really dead?"

"Yep. Killed on the bus to prison. The judge denied him bail and he was being moved for safety reasons. He was supposed to be transported alone, but there was a last-minute pickup that looks very planned to me, but that's above my pay grade."

"Good," Colin grunted.

Mari glanced up at him, not exactly surprised by his savage tone. He'd made it clear what he thought of Sewall. And fine, she hated him too. But it was still hard to reconcile that with the man she'd flown for years. The man she thought she'd known, had spent countless hours with. The facts about some of his life had been real. But the man behind the mask—she hadn't known that Gary at all. The one who'd pulled a gun on her with no issue, had planned to kill her and likely dump her where she'd never be found.

"Can you tell us what was on the flash drive?" Mari asked.

Camila glanced around as if she thought someone might overhear, even though it was just the three of them in Colin's house. Then she took off her jacket and sat at the island to face them. "Between us?"

They both nodded.

"I don't know everything, but since I've helped the DEA in the past, and because you've been claimed by Redemption Harbor Security as one of their own—"

"Well, I have flown them out of trouble before." Mari sniffed slightly. She *was* one of them as far as she was concerned. Unofficially.

Camila just grinned. "Exactly. My contact let me look at some of the files and filled me in as best he could. Sewall has been building an empire for years. It's a little terrifying how well he embedded himself in New Orleans society and beyond. And it will be no surprise to you two to know that he had more than a handful of judges in his pockets as well as law enforcement. Through blackmail mostly. And, if you watch the news later tonight, don't be surprised if a scandal about a certain Mississippi senator comes out concerning fraud and a whole lot of other nasty stuff. He's already making plans to resign."

"Wow."

"Yep. There's a lot more though. He'd basically created layers upon layers to insulate himself, to make it look like a new cartel was making moves so that it would never come back on him. He'd already made so much money with running drugs, artwork, guns and even people that it's insane he still wanted more."

"For some people, there is no such thing as enough. They're just greedy to their bones," Colin said.

Camila nodded, her expression grim. "Exactly."

"What about his daughter?"

"Heidi from Five C's? She hates him and is giving the DEA everything possible she can on him. She tried turning him in years ago, but he tossed her into a psychiatric hospital with the help of dirty judges, lawyers and medical *professionals*. Though I use that word lightly." Camila's tone was filled with disgust. "There are a lot of people who are going to go down because of this. Some might get away, but a lot of assholes will be going to jail."

"And Ackerman just shoved that USB in my backpack? Why?"

"We don't know for sure since no one can ask him. But the theory is that he knew that he was being watched so he hid it in your backpack. Which makes sense. Maybe he'd planned to get it from you later. Sewall admitted to the DEA that Ackerman took something from him. Files. Says that he copied something off his hard drive and left a trail. And the only person he was with after he did it was you. And since Sewall's men couldn't find anything on Ackerman's person, he had someone search your place. When that didn't give him anything, he sent people after you."

"What about the two people in custody? The hired guns. Are they going to be a problem for Mari?" Colin asked.

"Oh, no, I almost forgot. They're dead too. Killed in holding. It's clear that Sewall made a lot of powerful enemies over the years and someone is cleaning house. The DEA isn't a hundred percent sure who's behind the killings, but they have a good idea it's linked to a cartel. And it won't come back on you."

Well that was something. "And hiring me was just part of his elaborate cover?"

"Seems so. You were essentially part of his surface life. He was a political consultant who flew all the time, worked with a reputable pilot, gave to charity, yada yada. And clearly he built his cover well—that life was *real*. He just happened to have another life where he made money off the pain of others. From what I've been hearing, people he's worked with for years are shocked about what's coming out about him. I have a feeling there's going to be a documentary about his double life one day."

That wasn't something Mari had any interest in, but she said, "Thank you for filling us in. Will his daughter be okay?" She'd heard from Bradford that the woman had been over-the-top rude, but it made sense now. Sewall had forced her to work for him, had basically controlled her entire life. And his loving wife? That had been a lie he'd told Mari years ago. His wife had died in a car accident when his daughter was six. Who knew if it had been an accident at all.

"I hope so. She's been incredibly cooperative. Seems she hated him more than anyone. No wonder." Camila shook her head slightly. "I have a feeling she'll end up in WITSEC and start over. Who knows." She slid off the chair and grabbed her jacket. "I'm going to let you both rest but reach out if you need anything. And if you want help planning Magnolia's baby shower, let me know. You've had a lot going on."

"You're the best, and I will." She hugged her friend, then turned to Colin, feeling completely drained. "Can I give you a gentle hug?"

"Always." He wrapped his arms around her oh so softly and she was careful not to hold him as hard as she wanted.

"It feels like it's really over," she whispered.

"Yeah. Though we still have to tell your brothers about us."

She looked up at him. “We’re waiting.”

“Fine. Sneaking around might be kind of fun.” He paused, his smile fading. “Once I can actually do anything physical, anyway.”

“Six to eight weeks!”

“It’ll be sooner than that.” Determination stamped his expression.

She scoffed lightly. “We’ll see what your doctor says.”

He just grinned. “We will see.”

Yeah, and she was going to win this one, because no way was she letting him do anything to screw up his recovery. Even if she had to threaten him with Kim justice to make him behave.

CHAPTER 41

Five weeks later

"I can't believe how many people are here," Magnolia whispered to Mari as they sat together.

"You have a bigger circle of people now." Mari put her hand on Magnolia's bump, hoping to feel a kick. Magnolia had told her that she had perpetual permission to touch her stomach any time she wanted. Best friend rules. "And I'm looking forward to spoiling this nugget so much. And you."

"You're the best." Magnolia put her hand over Mari's as Mari laid her head on Magnolia's.

"Okay, smile, you two! This is so cute I can't stand it." Abigail, Magnolia's mom, had her phone up to take a picture of them as she passed by the fireplace where they were sitting.

Mari's smile came easy when she was with her best friend.

"So when are you going to tell your family about you and Colin?" Magnolia's voice was pitched low, but Mari still glanced around.

Thankfully no one was paying attention to them, but Magnolia was right, this place was packed. Mari had ended up throwing the baby shower here at Magnolia and Ezra's home so they wouldn't have to transport all their gifts—of which there were many.

The entire Redemption Harbor crew was there, along with a lot of Magnolia and Mari's childhood friends. Not to mention people Magnolia had worked with in the past, of course Camila, some crossover pilot friends of theirs, her mom's friends and even Mari's parents, who loved Magnolia. It was like a who's who of New Orleans society.

Camila slid in next to them, her expression dry. "All right. You know I love y'all, but there are some fancy people here."

Magnolia snickered. "It's all my parents' friends." Frowning, she looked around. "Where is Ezra and everyone?"

And by everyone, Mari knew she meant the Redemption Harbor Security people. "Oh, they're outside by the pool playing some baby-themed game that Berlin made up. They're throwing a baby doll at the cornhole trying to get the head inside. Pretty sure Ezra is winning."

Magnolia looked at Mari in horror, then burst out laughing. "I don't know if that's a good thing or not, but I'm going to head out there."

"I'll go with you." Camila popped up before Magnolia had even finished.

"I'll be out there in a minute. I've got to find my own man." Mari stood with her, helping Magnolia to her feet even though Magnolia swore she didn't need a hand.

It took Mari some time to find Colin, but eventually found him in the laundry room of all places. "What are you doing in here?" she asked as she shut the door behind herself.

"Someone said we needed another case of water."

"You're not supposed to be lifting anything yet."

He gave her a dry look. "I know. I didn't think about it until I got in here."

"Promise?"

He laughed, his eyes crinkling slightly at the edges, and god, she loved the sound of his laugh. "I swear. I'm listening to the stupid doctor."

"She's not stupid." Mari hopped up onto the washing machine.

"I know, but it makes me feel better to say it. I'm just tired of not being able to do everything I want. With you, in case that wasn't clear," he added.

Spreading her thighs, she reached for him. "It was clear. But we can at least make out." Pretty much all they were doing until next week when he should get his final okay from his wonderful doctor.

"I can get on board with that." His voice dropped a couple octaves as he slid in between her legs, wrapped his arms around her.

She loved the feel of him holding her, though they'd had to be careful over the last month, plus. "Good, because—" She turned at the sound of the door opening and stared at her two brothers standing there, wide-eyed.

Evan's mouth dropped open.

Joseph blinked.

They were only a couple years apart but might as well be twins.

"Say one stupid word and I'll rip your faces off!" Mari shouted, her defensive instincts kicking in. She loved her brothers but they'd always been stupidly overprotective and today wasn't the day. Colin had saved her life. And even if he hadn't, she loved him more than she'd ever thought possible. She also knew that he loved her brothers, her family, and it would cut him deep if they reacted poorly.

Colin tightened his grip on her. "Your sister and I are together. I love her very much and I'm not asking for approval, but I hope you'll be accepting of our relationship. If you're not, that's a you problem, because this is happening." There was a hard edge to his voice, one she'd only heard once before.

It sent a thrill down her spine, but then to her surprise, her brothers groaned practically in unison.

"What's that for?" she demanded, ready to tackle them. She didn't care how old they were, she could still take them.

"We owe Carmen a hundred bucks each," Evan muttered. "She told us you two were together, that she'd seen a spark when we visited you a few weeks ago. But I thought you both were just working your way to finally getting together."

"So is Carmen right? How long have you guys been together?" Joseph asked.

"Since none of your business," Colin growled.

Which just made them laugh uproariously, much to Mari's surprise.

Carmen stuck her head around the corner, grinned at the two of them. "I knew it! Finally. You guys are perfect together and you'll be coming over for dinner tomorrow night."

"Ah—"

"Just say yes. I'm making empanadas."

"Oh, we'll be there," Mari said, looking up at Colin, who simply grinned down at her.

Then he kissed her, making her brothers groan obnoxiously but at least they left them in peace.

"So the cat's out of the bag," she said, pulling back.

"For the record, I never wanted this particular cat in any bag." His jaw tightened.

"I know, but thank you." She'd been sure of her feelings for him, but deep down she'd been terrified that his feelings had been based on all the intensity surrounding them. She hadn't wanted to tell everyone—meaning her family—only for them to break up days later.

She knew it was stupid but she'd needed that little buffer. Because apparently she was still learning to deal with all her emotions.

"Come on, let's go see what's going on out back. I heard something about games and cupcakes."

"You don't even like cupcakes." Which was a crime in itself as far as she was concerned.

"Yes, but you do, so come on." He slid his fingers through hers, proudly holding on to her as they stepped out into the hallway.

Thankfully they were able to avoid her brothers and made it outside unscathed to find that yep, a weird baby doll tossing game was happening. She could only imagine what her and Magnolia's parents' wealthy friends would think of all this and chuckled to herself at the thought.

"Who's winning?" she asked Berlin as she and Colin slid up next to them.

Gino and Ollie were outside too, Magnolia having invited them since they were friends with Colin and she'd wanted him to have friends here. Which of course she did, because Mari's best friend was wonderful.

And Mari had discovered that the hot redhead she'd seen leaving Colin's place all those weeks ago had been Gino's sister—and they hadn't been sleeping together nor had they ever been anything other than friends. The woman had left a bar at two in the morning upset because she'd caught her boyfriend (now ex) cheating on her and hadn't wanted to go home because she lived with Gino (and hadn't wanted him to know he'd been right all along about her ex). So she'd gone to Colin, a man who was like a brother to her.

"Rowan by two points, but I have a plan," Berlin whispered.

"Those are some seriously creepy dolls," Colin murmured as he eyed the playing area.

"Right? They look like they came from a haunted house."

"We found them in the attic of our place." Bear, Colin's brother, appeared out of nowhere, a beer in his hand, his fiancée Valentine at his side.

"And you didn't want to put them in a display case?" Mari asked Valentine as she hugged her.

"I suggested we salt and burn them." Her tone was dry as she stepped back.

Which just made Mari laugh as she hugged Bear. She loved that he'd found someone as nice as him. They were two adorable peas in an adorable pod.

"So you two are official?" Bear asked, looking between the two of them. He and Valentine already knew about them since they'd been over at Colin's place as much as she had the last month.

"Yep." Colin slid an arm around her shoulders, and oh, she wanted to burrow into him, wrap her whole body around him and just love him.

His doctor's okay to return to physical activity couldn't come soon enough. He wasn't the only one ready to get back in the saddle.

"So who here knew that Bradford is married?" Berlin called out as Rowan started to toss another baby doll.

The Victorian-era doll went wild, its creepy eyes seeming to see everything as it landed in a nearby bush.

"Ha, now you're behind." Berlin cackled as she plucked up the doll.

"Wait, Bradford, you're married?" Rowan demanded as he, Tiago, and Ezra all turned to stare at him. "To who?"

"I'm going to kill you." Bradford chucked another of the dolls at Berlin but he was laughing as he did. "What happened to having my back?"

"You narced me out to Chance last week, so now we're even."

"Oh my god, who are you married to?" Tiago asked.

Mari heard him say the name "Hope" right before the other three men lost it. Then the three of them basically herded Bradford back toward the pool, all talking over each other.

"I think this is enough drama for one day. I'm ready to leave if you are," she said to Colin. The truth was, she could have stayed another hour, but she could see the exhaustion creeping in on him.

He might be almost physically "fine" but he'd been stabbed and it had taken a toll on him. She had a feeling it was going to be longer than eight weeks before he was a hundred percent back to himself. So until then, and even afterward, it was her job to look out for him. Because he was always looking out for her.

He leaned down, brushed his mouth over hers. "I'm ready, but I'll grab you some cupcakes before we head out."

His words sent a little shiver down her spine. He was definitely her wingman for life.

EPILOGUE

I love you as high as airplanes fly.

Two months later

"I love being up here with you." Colin had flown for work, but today was the first time he'd been up in the air with Mari just because it was the perfect day. The sun had set fifteen minutes ago and they were still in that twilight stage where it wasn't completely dark out yet.

"Same." She spoke over her headset, pure joy in her face as she looked down at the water, still visible as they headed up the coast.

They'd spent the day together, just the two of them, stopping at a couple airports for gas, lunch, shopping, and now they were headed home. She'd basically moved in with him, but he wanted something permanent.

Mari was the one, something he'd known for a while. Now he just wanted to make it official. And even though he was relatively sure she'd say yes… Okay, maybe he wasn't. He had no doubt that she loved him.

She showed him every day.

But this was a big step for both of them, two people who'd been perpetually single for most of their lives. Both of their "great loves" were airplanes.

They really were meant to be together.

"Hey, there's something going on over there." She pointed. "I can't make out what it is."

He turned the airplane toward the little uninhabited island because he knew exactly what it was. As he flew, he dropped their elevation to about a thousand feet so their approach would be crystal clear.

"Oh my god!" Mari gasped as he flew lower, making sure her side of the plane faced the island and the strategically placed battery-powered candles that spelled out *Will you marry me, Mari?* Some of his friends and her friends had spent the last few hours setting everything up for them. He owed all of them for such a huge undertaking.

"Is that…" She looked over at him, and in the dimness of the cockpit he could see tears glittering in her eyes.

"Marry me?" he asked, fear and elation pumping through him, the milliseconds seeming to go on forever as he pulled out the ring he'd been holding on to.

"Yes!" She grinned at him, looking as if she was ready to jump him as he slid the simple band onto her finger. Mari would hate something flashy, so he'd gone with his instincts and selected a simple gold band with two engraved airplanes. Cheesy? Probably, but he didn't care. They could be cheesy together.

"I should have thought this through better," he growled before he leaned over, gave her a quick kiss. Because they couldn't do anything until they were firmly on the ground.

"No, this is perfect." She looked at the band, then back at him. "You're perfect. I love you so much."

"I love you too." He heard his phone pinging through his Bluetooth headset, knew it was his friends from the ground texting to ask about the proposal, but he'd get back to them later.

She looked back at the island as he flew a little lower, showing off for everyone below even though he couldn't see them. "You've really set yourself up now. I don't know how you compete with something like this."

"I plan on spending the rest of my life one-upping myself for you." Because she deserved the best.

"Okay now I'm crying for real." She batted away her tears as she leaned in, kissed him again, just briefly. "Now let's get back to the hangar and get naked."

"Hell yeah. We can officially break your plane in."

And start the rest of their lives.

Dear Readers,

Thank you for reading Fighting for Mari. Many of you will know that I've been taking flying lessons (and I'm officially a student pilot!) over the last ten months. I believe I've mentioned it in at least one of my newsletters and on social media that I passed my FAA knowledge test (written exam). I'm slowly getting my flight hours in as I work toward eventually getting my certification. So it should come as no surprise that I had to write about pilots. I've learned so much in the short time I started flying and have met so many incredible people who are so giving of their time and knowledge. I've been in the publishing industry for almost two decades, and writers in general are almost always open with their knowledge (I'm specifically talking about the romance industry since that's the one I'm directly involved in). So it was a pleasant surprise to find that the aviation industry is the same (in my limited experience). I'd always heard that pilots have big egos but my experience is that pilots are laid back and almost never brag about themselves. Every cool thing I've found out about pilots I've met, have come from other people talking about their accomplishments.

After my discovery flight, one of my CFIs told me I should join Women in Aviation International – so I did! And then, one of my other CFIs ended upstarting a local WAI chapter, which I'm now also involved in. So if this book feels like a love letter to aviation, it's because it is! I feel like I've walked into an entirely new world and am learning something new every single day because of it. And I can't help but share that love with my readers. I say this all the time, but it bears repeating; if you're thinking about trying something new in your life, do it sooner than later because absolutely nothing is guaranteed. Especially not time. For my fellow aviation buffs, if you haven't joined Women in Aviation International or The Ninety-Nines, please check them out. They are great organizations for women, and you will find yourself in great company.□

Sincerely,
Katie

ACKNOWLEDGEMENTS

First I owe a huge thank you to Allison Lensink, one of my CFIs (and now a friend!) for going above and beyond to help me with the little aviation details in this book. It goes without saying that any mistakes are my own. I tried to make this as realistic as possible but at the end of the day, I'm human. But Allison went out of her way to help me and I'll be forever grateful. I'm also grateful to Mark Stevens (LtCol, USAF, ret.) for all his knowledge in general and for the encouragement to join Women in Aviation. While he didn't directly advise on this book, he's passed on more knowledge and information than I hope to retain. For my editor, Julia, thank you again for helping keep this world in order. I'm grateful you care about things like time of day, the timeline, characters' ages, etc, LOL. You keep me on track! Tammy, thank you for line edits and that final polish. Sarah, thank you for all the things you do (always, forever). Jaycee, thank you for another wonderful cover! For my readers, thank you all for continuing to read this series and especially Tammy H. and Shelley C. for always sending me notes of things they find that need attention. And of course, to my wonderful pups Jack and Piper, thank you for being the best writer pups in existence.

ABOUT THE AUTHOR

Katie Reus is the *USA Today* bestselling author of the Red Stone Security series, the Ancients Rising series and the Redemption Harbor series. She fell in love with romance at a young age thanks to books she pilfered from her mom's stash. Years later she loves reading romance almost as much as she loves writing it.

However, she didn't always know she wanted to be a writer. After changing majors many times, she finally graduated summa cum laude with a degree in psychology. Not long after that she discovered a new love. Writing. She now spends her days writing paranormal romance and action-packed romantic suspense.

COMPLETE BOOKLIST

Ancients Rising

Ancient Protector

Ancient Enemy

Ancient Enforcer

Ancient Vendetta

Ancient Retribution

Ancient Vengeance

Ancient Sentinel

Ancient Warrior

Ancient Guardian

Ancient Warlord

Darkness Series

Darkness Awakened

Taste of Darkness

Beyond the Darkness

Hunted by Darkness

Into the Darkness

Saved by Darkness

Guardian of Darkness

Sentinel of Darkness

A Very Dragon Christmas

Darkness Rising

Deadly Ops Series

Targeted

Bound to Danger

Chasing Danger

Shattered Duty

Edge of Danger

A Covert Affair

Endgame Trilogy

Bishop's Knight

Bishop's Queen

Bishop's Endgame

Holiday With a Hitman Series

How the Hitman Stole Christmas

A Very Merry Hitman

All I Want for Christmas is a Hitman

MacArthur Family Series

Falling for Irish

Unintended Target

Saving Sienna

Moon Shifter Series

Alpha Instinct

Lover's Instinct

Primal Possession

Mating Instinct

His Untamed Desire

Avenger's Heat

Hunter Reborn

Protective Instinct

Dark Protector

A Mate for Christmas

O'Connor Family Series

Merry Christmas, Baby

Tease Me, Baby

It's Me Again, Baby

Mistletoe Me, Baby

Red Stone Security Series®

No One to Trust

Danger Next Door

Fatal Deception

Miami, Mistletoe & Murder

His to Protect

Breaking Her Rules

Protecting His Witness

Sinful Seduction

Under His Protection

Deadly Fallout

Sworn to Protect

Secret Obsession

Love Thy Enemy

Dangerous Protector

Lethal Game

Secret Enemy

Saving Danger

Guarding Her

Deadly Protector

Danger Rising

Protecting Rebel

Redemption Harbor® Series

Resurrection

Savage Rising

Dangerous Witness

Innocent Target

Hunting Danger

Covert Games

Chasing Vengeance

Redemption Harbor® Security

Fighting for Hailey

Fighting for Reese

Fighting for Adalyn

Fighting for Magnolia

Fighting for Berlin

Fighting for Mari

Fighting for Hope

Sin City Series (the Serafina)

First Surrender

Sensual Surrender

Sweetest Surrender

Dangerous Surrender

Deadly Surrender

Verona Bay Series

Dark Memento

Deadly Past

Silent Protector

Linked books

Retribution

Tempting Danger

Non-series Romantic Suspense

Running From the Past

Dangerous Secrets

Killer Secrets

Deadly Obsession

Danger in Paradise

His Secret Past

The Trouble with Rylee

Falling for Nola

Tempted by Her Neighbor

Falling for Valentine

Paranormal Romance

Destined Mate

Protector's Mate

A Jaguar's Kiss

Tempting the Jaguar

Enemy Mine

Heart of the Jaguar

www.ingramcontent.com/pod-product-compliance
Lightning Source LLC
Chambersburg PA
CBHW032204280425
25875CB00019B/159
9781635564396